PRAISE FOR QUESTIONING YOUR WAY TO FAITH

"Kazmaier's delight at framing good questions, in seeking answers and in encouraging others to do the same is evident throughout this book. His experience in the university lecture theatre, in the scientific laboratory, in apologetics discussion, and simply around the dinner table talking with friends shines through. Kazmaier's creative, imaginative storytelling combining clear explanations and logical analysis will help the reader engage and wrestle with intellectual challenges on life's faith journey. A highly recommended book to read."

—Rick Wukasch, Oakville Associate Pastor, The Meeting House

"*Questioning Your Way to Faith* is a philosophical discussion that will fuel your desire to seek understanding. Kazmaier presents two sides to the timeless debate in a non-confrontational, easy going dialogue between two friends—a safe haven from which the difficult questions can be asked—a place where one can challenge the foundations of their faith without judgment. An intellectually stimulating read written with openness and honesty."

—Tricia Sheridan, Author of *Magdahlia's Medallion*

"*Questioning Your Way to Faith* is an intellectual treat for all, teen and adult alike, who are asking genuine questions, desiring genuine answers."

—Mike Burns, Youth Pastor, Southside Community Church

PRAISE FOR THE HALCYON DISLOCATION

"In a truly original sci-fi fantasy that literally transcends space and time, Kazmaier hurls readers into a world with shady morals, dubious friendships and exotic surroundings. It's one turn after another as this colonization epic unfolds."

—Robert McCallum, Dirctor/Writer of *Unearthly*

"In his first novel, Kazmaier combines the knowledge of the scientist with the imagination of the story teller. *The Halcyon Dislocation* is an incredible tale that seems frighteningly credible, thanks to its compelling insights into human nature. It's an adventure; one that progresses on the weighty consequences of moral choices made without regard to morality. This novel will leave you thinking about freedom; what it really is, and how to preserve it."

—Patricia Paddey, Freelance Writer

"In the great tradition of cautionary tales, *The Halcyon Dislocation* explores the intersection of faith and science when the world of its protagonist is turned upside down. Chilling and relevant, this story is a wild ride that shakes the foundation of its characters' faith and world view."

—Scott Weisbrod, *Experience Planner*

"A gripping story with great ideas and insightful characterization."

—Mark Jokinen, *Mark Jokinen Books*

"This novel deals with important issues for older teens and undergrads. The Christian message is clear and unambiguous, and the author avoids anything graphic or explicit. Though a bit rough around the edges, with too much "show" and not enough "tell", it is well enough written to be recommended to those who enjoy science fiction."

—*The Curious Presbyterian*

"I was drawn in by the author's vivid descriptions and imagination in this new world that is Middle Earth-like."

—**Lisa Hall-Wilson,** *Marantha News*

"For his first novel, Kazmaier does well at quickly getting the plot in motion and describing the new world. The science makes for good reading, too; perhaps no surprise, since Kazmaier is a working and teaching scientist. He makes dimension and time travel seem plausible and comprehensible."

—**Lloyd Rang,** *Faith Today*

"Throughout the novel there is a keen and vital sense of adventure and discovery with elemental forces at work, both in a material and metaphysical/religious sense. The interest level is sustained throughout."

—*Writer's Digest*

"The universe that the author creates is one that I can only best compare to Tolkien's epic … It's often a tall task for any author to portray a simple world around [its] main character, but in Tolkien fashion, Peter Kazmaier creates a vivid universe filled with multiple cultures, philosophies, character-types, and story-lines, all handled with care representative of someone who truly understands and loves the characters and universe that they have created. I give this novel 4 out of 5 stars, and highly recommend it."

—Confessions of a Dangerous Mind

QUESTIONING
Your Way to Faith

Learning to

DISAGREE

Without Being

DISAGREEABLE

PETER KAZMAIER

QUESTIONING YOUR WAY TO FAITH
Copyright © 2013 by Peter Kazmaier

For more information or to order additional copies, please contact:
Wolfsburg Imprints
2421 Council Ring Road
Mississauga, Ontario, Canada
L5L 1E5
http://www.peterkazmaier.com

ISBN: 978-1-77069-964-9

Word Alive Press
131 Cordite Road, Winnipeg, MB R3W 1S1
www.wordalivepress.ca

WORD ALIVE PRESS
Just Write!

Cataloguing in Publication information may be obtained through Library and Archives Canada.

Dedication

To Michael, Philip, and Darren. I am convinced that parents learn more from their children than they ever impart to them.

Table of Contents

Reason is our soul's left hand,
Faith her right; by these we reach divinity.
~John Donne

Foreword

"I wish some of the young people in the youth group I lead could have been part of that conversation." Such has often been my lament as I've driven away from one of my favorite bimonthly activities, aptly named on my calendar as "Lunch with Peter."

For more than a decade I have enjoyed a rich and meaningful friendship with Peter. With both a genuine, unique perspective on faith, and the ability to express difficult concepts in an understandable way, I was thrilled to see his first book *The Halcyon Dislocation* come to print. The imaginative plot line and fast paced action start on page one and don't stop until the book is complete. Masterfully interwoven throughout are the real questions of life, those big "God questions" that most ask but few get answers for. It is in working through such questions that Peter shines, as the dialogue between "Al and Floyd" demonstrates, bringing together fundamentally different views in the context of respectful conversation and friendship.

Understanding the conversational nature of teens and the pluralistic worldviews to which they are exposed, I recognized that Peter's ability to raise the big questions of life that teens are genuinely asking—and to provide meaningful answers—is a gift. For this reason I encouraged him to write the book you now hold in your hands: a continued dialogue between two friends, engaged in conversations that we all have likely had before, only with Peter's gifted mind and perspective to lead the way. Faith is not just an "idea" to Peter or a problem to be solved, but the foundation of a meaningful relationship with his Creator through the person of Jesus Christ.

Questioning Your Way to Faith is an intellectual treat for all, teen and adult alike, who are asking genuine questions, desiring genuine answers. I cannot always take my teens to "Lunch with Peter" but at least now I can take Peter to my teens.

Mike Burns, Youth Pastor
Southside Community Church

Author's Note

It is an axiom of polite conversation that politics and religion are two topics that must be scrupulously avoided. You will not find talk of politics in this book, but you will find pages filled with discussion about conflicting worldviews.

In my own experience, respectful conversations with friends with whom I had profound disagreements on the existence, nature, and role of God in our world, have been of paramount significance in helping me understand their most salient questions.

I realize these questions are not equally significant to everyone. For some the existence of God is wholly an intensely personal experience, and global questions such as: "What is the philosophical evidence for God?" and "Where does evil come from?" have little importance. If you find yourself thinking this way, then the questions this book discusses may hold little relevance for you. One can, of course, be a fulfilled and vibrant Christian without ever wrestling with such issues. However, even if these questions have little import for you, it may still be worth your while to grapple with them for the sake of others.

For many, the biggest questions of life are intellectual barriers that must be removed before genuine faith in God becomes possible. It is my hope and prayer that this book will be of value for such kindred spirits as these. Seek the truth. Respectfully dialogue with people who disagree. Keep questioning and seeking answers until you find them!

~ Peter Kazmaier

ONE

Questioning Your Way to Faith

"Next week," said Professor Stillman, "we will begin discussing the fascinating chemistry of indole alkaloids. In the interim, please read the handout. That's all for today."

Al Gleeson took off his glasses and rubbed his eyes. *I must be a real nerd to enjoy organic chemistry.* He closed his books and shuffled to the end of the row of lecture desks, then began the long climb to the back exit of the cavernous lecture hall. He could smell the faint, fragrant aroma of esters wafting in from the adjacent chemistry labs.

"Hey, Al."

Feeling a vague annoyance at having his thoughts interrupted, Al searched for the speaker at the back of the lecture hall. Seeing who it was, he brightened, then hurried to meet his friend, clapping him on the back. Floyd Linder was uncharacteristically subdued; his face had a gaunt, haunted expression. Al wondered what was up. His friend was every inch a leader and an athlete and normally looked the part. But today—the contrast made Al swallow hard.

"Floyd—where have you been?"

"I had to fly back home in a hurry."

"Excuse me," said a student, pushing past them to the exit.

Floyd ran his hand over his shaven head. Al could see his eyes were moist. "My grandmother died—passed away suddenly. I went back for the funeral."

Al swallowed hard. "I'm so sorry Floyd. I didn't know. You don't really look yourself. Now I know why."

"It shows, huh?"

"Yes it shows. Is your mother okay?"

Floyd shifted his weight and shoved his hands into his pockets. "It's hard to tell. On the outside she seems unruffled." The corners of Floyd's mouth turned into a stiff smile. "But then we Linders are known for our toughness."

"Excuse me," said another student, pushing past.

Floyd nodded his head toward the exit, then hitched his knapsack over one shoulder and walked out of the lecture hall toward the front entrance of the chemistry building. He stopped in front of the glass doors and high windows, staring wistfully out at the rocky, tree-clad pinnacle that dominated the skyline in the southwest corner of the Halcyon University island campus. "Listen Al, there's something that's been bothering me about this funeral, and I need someone to talk to. Do you have some time?" he asked, his eyes still fixed on the mountain in the distance.

Al hesitated and then felt guilty for hesitating. "Of course I have time. We can go for a walk."

"Want to take a walk toward the mountain?" asked Floyd. "There's less chance of interruptions there."

Outside, the sun was beaming and the air had the fragrance of spring. The broad promenade was a divided avenue that ran straight south toward South Mountain. Large flowerbeds, rock gardens and fruit trees dominated the center of the walkway. Al smelled apple blossoms. Floyd moved stolidly onwards, his hands jammed into his pockets and his head down.

"You must love your grandmother very much to grieve like this."

"I guess a lot of how I feel is grief, but there's something else that I have trouble putting into words."

"Could you try?" said Al.

"I don't know Al." Floyd took a brief sidewise glance toward him, and groped for words. "It's just that the funeral was more religious than I expected it to be."

"And that bothers you?"

"Yeah," said Floyd.

"I don't really understand why you would find that so unusual," said Al.

Floyd looked at Al as if making a decision and then took a deep breath. "To understand what surprised me about the funeral, you have to know a little bit about my family. Both my grandfathers and my father were very intelligent, realistic people who looked at the world the way it is," said Floyd. "I remember my grandfather, my mom's dad, telling me that he would believe in God the moment he saw evidence for him. He was really saying he'd never seen any evidence for God. My dad went further. He stated quite firmly that God doesn't exist."

"Go on," Al prompted.

"Well at the funeral, I wasn't that surprised that my grandmother had requested a church minister to officiate. I guess that's customary. But they read a letter she'd written in which she affirmed her faith not only in God, but in Jesus Christ—who I'd always just thought of as some dead carpenter who'd lived 2000 years ago. It floored me. All this time I thought she was with the program and believed as my grandfather did, and now I find out that's not true. Part of me says she just succumbed to wishful thinking at the end. But knowing her, I don't really believe it."

"So how can I help?"

"Well, I'm pretty sure you're a Christian," Floyd cleared his throat. "Yet you don't seem like a 'nut job'—sorry, I don't mean to give offence—so I thought I would ask you about what you believe. I didn't want to go to a professional Christian—like the minister at the funeral—because they would just proselytize me."

Al chuckled. "Well, I may yet be relegated to your 'nut job' bin after you hear some of the strange things I believe. But if I can help, I'd like to do whatever I can."

"Thanks," said Floyd. "Mind if I ask you a few personal questions?"

Personal questions? What's he going to ask me?

"Sure go ahead."

"You were raised a Christian, right?" Floyd asked.

"Not exactly," said Al. "My father was a Professor of Psychology and a Marxist. He detested all religion. He considered it the 'opiate of the masses.' My mother wanted to go to church, but he criticized her mercilessly until she gave it up." Al felt anger rising as he thought about it even after all these years. "I knew that and resented it. After my mother died and my father remarried, I eventually stood up to him and decided to go to church, more out of rebellion than conviction."

"Is that why you still go to church now?" asked Floyd.

"No, even if you grow up in the church, I'm pretty sure most everyone comes to the point where they begin to question their faith. That questioning happened to me. I didn't really become a Christian, that is a Christ-follower, by going to church. I was searching for the truth, and so I asked many questions. I questioned so much that I literally questioned my way to faith."

Floyd's eyebrows bunched together. "Questioned your way to faith? That doesn't make a whole lot of sense to me," said Floyd.

"Why do you find that so surprising?" asked Al.

"Questioning is what scientists do," said Floyd. I've always understood that science operates by experiment and observation but religion—especially Christianity—operates by faith. Saying that you 'questioned your way to faith' is an oxymoron. 'Faith' means accepting something as true because a god told you to and will punish you if you don't believe him."

Al stared at Floyd. "Does it?" asked Al. "A good deal turns on the definition of faith. If we want to talk about this we have to use the same definition for faith in order to have a meaningful conversation."

"I think the definition I'm using is pretty good and I've heard scientists use it before," said Floyd. "What's wrong with it?"

Passing a bed of bright yellow daffodils interspersed with red tulips Al paused to enjoy the beauty of the colorful display. He reached down to touch a delicate flower.

How beautiful! Uplifted, he pulled himself back to the question at hand.

"You're right," said Al. "Like you, I've heard that definition of faith before from scientists and even scientific organizations. It's usually advanced by scientists who are also Materialists, believing that the world consists *only* of matter and energy. They're outsiders defining faith for someone else in a way that suits their own cherished worldview. Defining faith as being commanded by a god and not linked to evidence or observation, conveniently allows them to keep the 'real'—by that they mean 'matter and energy'—for their worldview, and to relegate the mythical and illusory to 'faith.'"

"Maybe they're right," Floyd protested.

"Maybe they are. But it seems to me if you want to discuss what the Christian concept of faith means, you have to look at how Christians throughout the ages have defined it, and they get their definition from the New Testament."

"So what's the New Testament definition of faith?" asked Floyd.

"In the New Testament," said Al, "the Greek noun for faith can be transliterated *pistis*[1] while the verb for believe is the related word *pisteuo*."

"What's 'transliterated'?"

"Well Greek has its own alphabet. Transliterated means the Greek characters have been replaced by phonetically equivalent English letters." Al paused, allowing that thought to sink in. "So," he continued, "*pistis* when used for faith, literally means 'a conviction based on hearing.' Another sense of the word is trust."

"But isn't that what I said?" asked Floyd.

"Not exactly," said Al. "You said that 'faith' means accepting something as true because a god told you to and will punish you if you don't believe him. But here's the key point; unless one is completely naïve, one might be compelled *to mouth the words of agreement* to a powerful tyrant who demands belief and threatens punishment—the kind of threatening god you were talking about—but surely that very process is the antithesis of *conviction,* which requires freedom of thought."

Floyd rubbed the stubble on his chin. He searched Al's face. "So what you're saying is that a tyrant god may have sycophants who play at worshipping him and telling him what he wants to hear, but deep down

---

[1] W. E. Vine, *An Expository Dictionary of New Testament Words* (Old Tappan, Fleming H. Revell, 1966), p. 71.

most of those followers would know their response was coerced and that coercion is incompatible with conviction and faith." Al nodded. "Okay—that makes sense," said Floyd.

Floyd's really listening to me and trying to understand what I say. Not many people do that. They usually just wait for me to stop talking, so they can move on to their next sentence.

Al could feel himself getting excited. "I think you're getting the idea. But you also have to get into the mindset of people in the New Testament era to really understand how they viewed faith. For the ancients to base a conviction on what another person told them, that person had to prove their trustworthiness through action and also demonstrate an unshakeable commitment to the truth. In other words," said Al, "a close relationship is essential for faith. That's why trust is a synonym for faith. That's also why Christ, your 'carpenter of 2000 years ago,' spent three years with his disciples: so that they could see him in action through day-to-day contact, see his healing touch, his compassion for the poor, his anger with the heartlessness and hypocrisy of the religious leaders. Those actions showed his followers what he was like. He knew he had to build up trust through actions his disciples could see and verify so they could trust him for the things that were beyond observation. All along he gave concrete evidence of his trustworthiness to qualify himself in their eyes as a straight shooter—someone who would always tell them the truth."

"But couldn't a person be deluded in his beliefs and still have conviction and an unshakeable commitment to the truth?" asked Floyd.

"Sure," said Al, "If the messenger were honest but deluded, he would change his mind and correct his earlier statements once he found his error. But what I do rule out is the perspective that the messenger is a deceiver and knowingly misleads the audience. The ancients would look for evidence the messenger was reliable and honest before they listened to the message. That's not blind faith."

Floyd shook his head slowly. "Al, it still sounds to me as if faith and experiment are fundamentally different. In science, we base our conclusions on experiments. You religious guys go on trust or faith—whatever you want to call it."

"That's not really what I mean," said Al. He felt frustration beginning to grow.

How can I explain this? They were just passing the athletic complex and that gave Al an idea. "Sure faith and experiment may be different," Al responded, "but are they different in the sense of being contradictory? Or are they different in the sense of being complementary?"

"What do you mean Al?"

"Think about hockey," said Al.

"Hockey?"

"I forgot you North Carolina guys don't know about hockey," Al teased.

"I know about hockey. What's your point, Al?"

"Think about coming to a pickup hockey game with your friends and bringing a tennis racket instead of a hockey stick." said Al. "Would that work?" Al pretended to swipe at a hockey puck with a tennis racket to make his point.

"No, of course not."

"The differences between a tennis racket and a hockey stick are such that they make the tennis racket unsuitable for hockey."

Floyd chuckled. "Okay, captain obvious. Where are you going with this?"

"Well what about a hockey stick and a hockey puck?" said Al. "They're also different. Do you need them to play hockey?"

"Of course," Floyd said.

"Here's the point: there are two ways of being different. For lack of a better term, hockey sticks and tennis rackets are contradictory—they're in an either/or relationship. You'd pick one for tennis and the other for hockey, and they can't be interchanged. The hockey puck is also different, but it's different in a complementary sense. Both are essential to the game. I think Materialists assume faith and experiment are different in the contradictory sense, while I maintain they're different in the complementary sense."

Floyd thrust his hands into his pockets again. "Okay, let me see if I get your argument. You're admitting that faith and experiment are different, but you're insisting I need both even to study science, just like

I need a hockey stick and a hockey puck to play hockey. Why do I need faith to study science?"

"Floyd, when you learned the Ideal Gas Law, did you accept it as true because you worked it out yourself, or because a trusted person told you?"

"I did a lab on Charles' Law, but mostly I guess I accepted it because my prof taught it to me." Floyd shrugged. "But the law can't be wrong. Others have checked it, and we use it every day. It can't be wrong."

Al turned towards Floyd. "I'm not saying it is wrong. I'm saying most of what we learn—even in the sciences—we learn by faith and trust in the Christian sense of the words. We don't have the time, the equipment and, in some cases, we don't have the understanding to verify everything ourselves. We learn by believing the teachings of reliable people. Faith and observation are not opposites but complementary. Even when we do the actual experiments ourselves, we can't wholly escape faith since we have to trust our senses and our own competence. Our senses and our competence are not experimentally verifiable since any test we conduct on ourselves to test them, would depend on us using our senses and assuming our competence to evaluate the test results. So the core faculties we use to conduct and analyze our experiments—our mind and our senses—can't be validated by experiment since that would lead to a circular argument."

"Why is it a circular argument?"

"Well," said Al, "if I decide to conduct an experiment to determine whether my senses and my mind provide data that are representative of reality, I have to use my mind to design the experiment, and my senses to make the observations. So I'm already assuming they've been proven reliable. It's a circular argument and I'm 'begging the question.'"

"So you're saying that when I think about data as a scientist, or listen to a lecture from an expert, I'm actually exercising my faith?"

Al smiled broadly. "Exactly! So this idea, that faith is for the religious and observation is for the scientists and philosophical Naturalists, doesn't stand up to scrutiny. We all need faith, reason and observation to progress. All three are linked." Al linked the fingers of both hands together, emphasizing the point."

"Is this concept of yours—about faith and reason being complementary—a new idea?" asked Floyd.

"No it's not. Are you familiar with the English poet John Donne?"

"Yeah, I studied him in high school," said Floyd.

"I think Donne saw it clearly when he said, 'Reason is our soul's left hand, Faith her right; by these we reach divinity.'"[2]

The two friends walked along in silence for a few moments. The mountain—with its rocky crags breaking through the green cloak of the forest—loomed before them. Al glanced over at Floyd; he seemed to be deep in thought. His head was down and he was looking at his feet.

"Okay, let's work with your 'biblical' definition of faith, said Floyd at last. For the sake of argument, I'll accept that by the Christian definition, faith and experiment are not contradictory but complementary, and that at least some Christians exercise reason as they work out their philosophy of life. Given that, I can see that you questioned your way to faith. However it seems to me, that a faith position is still antithetical to doubt and skepticism. Most Christians, as far as I can tell, never ask questions. My conversations with Christians in the past consisted of listening to one long list of assertions designed to win me over."

"Okay, Floyd, why do you ask questions?" Al tossed the question and a pebble into the air.

---

[2] John Donne, *Poems of John Donne.* Vol II, E. K. Chambers, ed. (London, Lawrence & Bullen, 1896), p15.

TWO

The Importance of Questions

"Why do I ask questions?" Floyd asked catching the pebble Al had tossed. "I suppose I'm naturally skeptical of the assertions that people make, and I want to get to the bottom of things. Why do you ask questions, Al?"

"Questions are really important," Al replied. "When you ask a question you believe there have to be answers. To the ancients, the idea of genuine answers implied there was objective truth linked to reality. If reality is defined as 'those things that don't go away just because you stop believing in them,' then answers matter."

"But Al, don't you agree that there are people who never seem to ask questions? They just make assertions?"

"I do Floyd, and that tendency is not just restricted to Christians. I think there are two kinds of people who never ask honest questions: those who believe they already have all the answers, and those who believe there are no answers."

"How does that work, Al?"

"Well there are some who claim there is no such thing as objective truth. Everything is semantics and feelings masquerading as truth. If you believe that, you won't ask questions because you're convinced there are no answers. Or at least, the answers are on the level of taste. 'I think red is a nicer color than blue.'

"I think I've met people like that," said Floyd. "I guess I wouldn't have called them dishonest because they're genuinely convinced there are no answers to fundamental questions and they just ask questions to bring people into conversation."

"Hmm, I see your point Floyd. When I said 'honest questions,' I meant genuine questions directed at finding genuine answers. I think you're right that there are some people who are honestly convinced there are no answers, but they ask questions as a verbal construct, a tool to bring people into conversation. As I think of it, don't you see the internal contradiction in that philosophy of absolute relativism? These people can't really operate without absolutes or without questions that have absolute answers. I'm sure these thoroughgoing relativists look both ways before crossing the street since the answer to the question 'Is a bus coming?' is as important to their survival as it is to mine. Even on the philosophical front, they hold at least one absolute truth—there is no such thing as an absolute truth!"

"I'm not a relativist, Al, so with your clarification we're now on the same page. You were talking about the second kind of people who never ask any questions. Who are they?"

"The second group of people is the polar opposite of the relativists. If your level of conviction in all areas is absolute, then again you won't ask genuine questions, because you already know all the answers. I didn't have answers so I asked questions. Lots of them. First I tried to answer the questions myself. Then I talked to people I trust. Finally I read a lot of books, which is like talking to people *in absentia*. All three of these approaches helped me a lot."

Floyd brightened, stuffing his hands into his pockets. "I've met some of those people who think there are no answers. They make me feel like I don't belong, or that we have little basis for understanding. I'm surprised that you and I—despite our conflicting ideas about the world and spirituality—have a lot in common. More than I expected. I always figured Christians would consider questions and questioning as an attack on their faith. It actually feels good to have someone to talk to about this—someone who won't get angry because my questions are too difficult for them to handle."

Al could see Floyd was trying to suppress a smile.

He's trying to get a reaction out of me. It's just not going to happen!

Al tried to put on the most serious expression he could. "I can see why you might think that Floyd. I mean the part about questions being an attack on faith. These topics on God and the nature of reality hit close to home and can threaten the very foundations of our thinking and how we view the world. So getting angry and feeling threatened is always a danger."

"Let's not do that," said Floyd. "Get angry I mean."

"I agree. Your thought brings me to another thing I've learned on this journey. I guess I'm a rather odd character. I ask a lot of questions that many of my friends—both Christian and Agnostic—don't care about and so never ask. Finding someone who's bothered by the same questions I am about the nature of reality is like finding gold. Respectful dialogue between friends is a cornerstone of finding out the truth. I think that whatever our differences may be in how we look at reality, we care about the same kinds of questions. That's why I value our conversation so much.

"But this digression on faith aside, we should get back to your initial topic. So Floyd, do you have a sense of what's bothering you?"

"The faith my grandmother and you share bothers me."

"Can you elaborate?" Al probed.

Floyd rubbed his chin. "I guess it comes down to how I feel about my grandmother's religious views and yours. Let me see if I can put it into words."

Floyd walked on quietly. Finally he looked at Al and said, "One thing puzzles me about you, Al…"

He started again. "I don't know quite how to say this. Okay, you're a bright guy. You've studied the sciences like I have. I don't understand how you can be so religious. If you believed in a universal spiritual force, life-spirit or Gaia, I would disagree but I would understand where you're coming from. But going beyond that by believing in the God of the Jews, a being with a mind who has made the world out of nothing, is even more repugnant to me because I think you're projecting human characteristics onto God. But you don't even stop there. You go beyond that, believing that Christ, this Jewish carpenter is God, as if this universe-creating God would care enough about us to show up on our speck of a planet and walk around as a human being. To me that's so preposterous—it's like believing in Santa Claus."

Al looked at Floyd. "I think Floyd, you're grappling with the enormity of the event that Christians call the Incarnation. You're not alone in your amazement."

"For me," said Floyd, 'It's not really amazement but repugnance. When I ask myself 'Why am I reacting this way?' I guess the answer is that I believe science has disproven religion. Fundamentally I think science and religion are incompatible."

"Why do you say that? How has science disproven religion?"

"Well," said Floyd, "I've lived my whole life without religion. I know where I come from, where the universe comes from. Everything I know about myself is explained by science. Without religion I'm just fine, so where's the need for it? What good is it really? If I can explain everything without it, it seems to me religion's like a vestigial organ—useless and on its way out."

"Floyd, to me the question of first importance isn't 'What good is it?' but rather 'Is it true?' Still I can see your point about having explanations for everything without faith in God. But the idea that *everything* can be explained by observation and experimentation isn't a scientific idea. It's a philosophical or metaphysical idea. It's naturalism or materialism," said Al.

"Why isn't it a scientific idea?" asked Floyd.

"Well," said Al, "the assumption that *everything* can be explained by experiment—or through natural cause and effect processes—can't be verified by experiment. The most you can do with this philosophical position is to try it out to see how internally consistent it is."

"Okay," said Floyd, "in your language, I've tried naturalism and it explains everything. So what use is faith in God?"

"If you accept as true the view that our whole world consists of matter, energy and laws that govern physical behavior, then you can form a philosophically closed system. That is to say, you can explain some things about our world and the people in it well, and other things that don't fit, you explain away."

"I happen to think everything fits. What sorts of things don't fit?"

"The sorts of things that don't fit are questions such as: why have almost all people been religious if faith in a god is so out of tune with our world? Why are we conscious of morality if our whole world consists only of matter and energy? What makes us rational? Where does inferential thought come from? Why do we have this sense that we want to live forever and why are we distressed when we become conscious of our own mortality? Why do I have a sense that there is a real me apart from my body? I watch a cardinal in my back yard. Why do I find the plumage on the bird beautiful? In fact where does the idea of beauty come from at all?"

"Whoa," said Floyd. "Not so fast. You're machine-gunning me with your list. Still, I think I have explanations for all of these things. For example, beauty can be explained as a disguised version of the sexual impulse."

Al smiled. "Does 'disguised sexual impulse' *really* explain my point about finding the plumage of a cardinal beautiful?" asked Al. "Wouldn't it be fairer to say naturalism has a way of explaining these problems *away* rather than explaining them? It seems to me, looking at naturalism from the outside in, I wouldn't have expected any of these things to arise if natural laws, matter, and energy were the only building blocks. In naturalism, people are chemical machines driven only by the impulse to survive and reproduce. To me that explanation doesn't really tell me why I should find a cardinal or a daffodil beautiful."

"I come back to my point," said Floyd, "which I don't think you've adequately addressed. Why do people like me get along just fine without believing in God or religion?"

"First of all," said Al, "I *do not* think naturalism or even *most religions* explain our world and the people in it equally well. The best we can do from an intellectual point of view is place religious and philosophical systems side by side to see which one seems to offer the best explanation.

"Fair enough," said Floyd.

"For me," continued Al, "theism, particularly Christian theism, is the best explanation intellectually. As a Christian, I also have personal experience that provides a different, experiential, and personal line of verification. For some, the mystical or experiential aspect is all they need or want. I personally want both."

"Okay, Al, that's a roundabout way of saying that you're a Christian because you believe it to be true."

"Right," said Al. "Back to your question. Naturalism isn't wholly wrong. You see the world clearly. Science *can* answer many kinds of questions, and you take those answers as evidence in favor of your worldview. But theism, the idea that there is a personal God who created the whole world out of nothing and sustains it, also accepts the questions that science can answer as support for the *theistic worldview*. Looking at science really does not discriminate between the two worldviews."

Floyd stopped, turned to Al and folded his arms across his chest. "I think you're dodging a big problem Al. I'd say that religions, including Christianity, had very different views about the solar system, the earth, the human body and living things in general *until corrected by science*. You're just reinterpreting and re-inventing your religion to fit what science says today. Sure once science has told us the earth is round or has worked out celestial mechanics, then you find a way of rationalizing the results and making it compatible with the Bible. I don't have to do that. I simply accept science for what it says and that's it. I follow the evidence wherever it leads unencumbered by the restrictions of religious teaching."

Al grimaced. "I see your point. It's true that people in times past have believed things about our world that later, more careful observation proved untrue or incorrect. But don't you see? People have *always brought* their view of the world to their interpretation of the Bible. If Euclid showed farmers and cartographers how to use plane geometry to survey their fields, of course people would naturally think the world is flat because their local observations are consistent with a flat world. They didn't get this *from the Bible*, they brought it *to the Bible*."

"But my point is," said Floyd, "that Christians are constantly adjusting their views to the findings of science."

"But Naturalists are also adjusting their views of the world according to what science finds experimentally," said Al. "The difference is that when that adjustment occurs, Naturalists say 'Science is wonderful. It brings me closer and closer to the truth as I modify my view about the world.' When Christians engage in the *very same process*, it is somehow taken as evidence against their faith."

"So where does that leave us, Al?"

"Floyd, I would say all truth is God's truth, so one is always reconciling what one 'knows' about the world by observation with our interpretation of the scriptures. The trouble is that what one 'knows' about the world is continually being refined.

"Floyd, I think one of the great dishonesties of naturalism is that it's a worldview that strongly identifies with science and *denies that same identification* to other worldviews. Naturalism takes the credit for *all* of the accomplishments of science. It does this even though science flourished most strongly in the fertile soil of Christian Europe and North America and many of the contributors—in fact just about all of the early contributors—held a Judeo-Christian worldview."

"But Al, what about my point that people like me can simply take science as it is without any adjustment or rationalization. Isn't that more honest or straightforward?" Floyd asked.

"More honest and straightforward? I don't see it," said Al.

"Why not?"

Al ran his hand through his hair. "Naturalism is centered on the observable," he said, "so any observation is embraced. But naturalism only allows certain kinds of explanations for all of these phenomena. Everything has to be explained mechanistically by physical laws. There's no room for the supernatural. It's true, Naturalists don't have a sacred text that has to be rationalized, but at every point they must strenuously defend against any evidence or anecdote that hints at the supernatural.

"For example, many Christians can relate anecdotes of remarkable, highly improbable personal events they have experienced, which they believe show evidence for God's operation in their lives. All these personal events must be debunked by a thoroughgoing Naturalist, since if even one of them were true, they would cause the whole naturalist worldview to be unhinged.

"Therefore you have a different kind of rationalization going on all the time: a debunking of every answer to prayer, every experience of the presence of God, every idea that our whole universe is more than the consequences of the mindless vibrations of atoms."

"Well, that was quite a mouthful," Floyd said, "but you've given me a lot to think about. I'm going to need some time to process this." He pointed ahead at the 3,000-foot mountain rising steeply before them. "Should we continue on or call it a day?"

The clouds had begun to roll in. The air was pregnant with the smell of imminent rain.

"Yes Floyd, we should break it off. I'd love to continue, but I have to head back to the library. You've given me plenty to think about too."

"Sure thing. I've got to head to the dorm. I've got a lot of catching up to do. Shall we get together for breakfast tomorrow morning? Say 6:15?"

"Sure tomorrow at breakfast would work for me," said Al.

Al found himself whistling on the way to the library.

Wow. Floyd and I have very different answers to some of these tough questions, but I think I've found a kindred spirit. So few of my Christian friends care about these questions the way I do. It's good to find a thinker who searches for the truth.

THREE

The Problem of Evil

Al entered the cafeteria at 6:00 a.m. The staff had that bleary-eyed look of those who had not had enough sleep. He selected a generous helping of scrambled eggs and added a mound of hash browns and two slices of bacon from the cafeteria line food station. The smell of bacon made him realize how hungry he was. He added a couple of sausages to his plate.

Breakfast has always been the best meal they prepare in this cafeteria.

He scanned the many free tables and saw Floyd sitting in a corner by a window. As he approached the table, Floyd looked up and broke into a broad smile.

"And I thought I was early," said Al. "You look tired."

"Thanks for the morning compliment Al. I hope I don't look as bad as the zombie cafeteria workers at this time of the morning. Still you have to come early to get the best seat in the house."

"I wasn't trying to insult you."

Floyd laughed. "None taken. But seriously, my mind has been buzzing after our conversation yesterday. I didn't get much sleep. I've been thinking about what you said. It sort of made sense, but the worry nagged me that there must be something wrong."

Al sat down and took a sip of coffee. "Were you able to figure out what was bothering you?"

Floyd leaned forward eagerly. "I was sent to Vacation Bible School as a kid when my parents needed a break in the summer. I learned that

God is supposed to have these infinite properties. He's supposed to be all-knowing, and all-powerful. He's also supposed to be good."

"I think you're talking about the three 'omnies': omnipotent, omniscient, and omnipresent," said Al.

"The three 'omnies'? What are you talking about?" asked Floyd.

"Sorry, Floyd. The 'omnies' are three terms theologians have coined to describe God. They're not actually used in the Bible, but they refer to properties of God that the Bible describes and illustrates with examples."

"So what are the definitions?"

"Well," said Al, "at the risk of oversimplifying, 'omnipotent' means that God has the power to do all things, 'omniscient' means he knows all things, and 'omnipresent' means he is present everywhere. I think these qualities are the qualities you're remembering from Vacation Bible School, and they cause us problems of comprehension because they're infinite properties."

"Yeah whatever. Okay if God really has these properties, how do you explain the sorry state of our world? How can an all-powerful God create a world that contains so much evil? If God exists and evil exists, then he can't be both *all-good* and *all-powerful*. If he were all-good, then the existence of evil means he would like to fix things, but can't stop the evil. If he has the power to stop it and won't, then God is not truly good.

"We hear about children dying, natural disasters that kill thousands. Acts of terrorism that kill innocent bystanders. Look at my case." Floyd shifted in his seat. "Sure my grandmother lived a long time and had a good life. But why does her passing have to cause me so much pain? If there is a God, he's either standing on the sidelines indifferent to our pain or he actually enjoys it because he's a cosmic sadist. Do you see my problem?"

"Yes, I see it your point."

"For me then," continued Floyd, "the simple solution to this dilemma is to affirm that God does not exist and so this problem goes away."

Al buttered a piece of toast as he tried to put his thoughts together.

How do I address this so that I make sense?

"You're right Floyd," Al said at last. "The problem of evil is, I think, the most difficult question about God's nature that faces Christians. The difficulty hits us all personally sooner or later at an emotional level, whether it's the death of a loved one, a natural disaster that affects us, or simply the pervasive injustice that confronts us. Even Christians who've worked through some of the principles that help us deal with this problem, still have to work through it all over again when evil and calamity strike their personal lives."

"Okay, Al so what's the answer?"

"What's the answer? It's complicated…"

"I'm listening," said Floyd.

Al picked up his other piece of toast and began to butter it as meticulously as the first.

"I read a book by Peter Kreeft, a Professor of Philosophy at Boston College, and his colleague Ronald Tacelli[3] that helped me a lot. According to Kreeft and Tacelli, they discuss this problem in terms of four propositions.

Al took a napkin and wrote down four points:

1. God exists
2. God is supremely good
3. God is supremely powerful
4. Evil exists

"Another way of stating the apparent contradiction you pointed out, Floyd, is to say that all four propositions can't be true at the same time. Once three are true, the fourth proposition must be false."

"You're losing me Al."

"Okay, let me give you some examples of how this works. As an Atheist, you deny the first proposition that God exists, so two and three become irrelevant, and you're left with proposition four that *evil exists*. By denying the first proposition on the existence of God you've removed the contradiction and have an explanation for evil."

---

[3] Peter Kreeft and Ronald K. Tacelli, *Handbook of Christian Apologetics* (Downers Grove, IVP Academic, 1994), p. 128-133.

"Back to the original question," said Floyd, "How you get around the dilemma we talked about? The four propositions in your argument seem watertight to me. What's your answer, Al?"

"Well the simple answer is that Christians affirm that *all four propositions are true.*"

"How can that be? That makes no sense."

"Let me try to explain Kreeft and Tacelli's argument. Our four-proposition argument can only be invalid if at least one of three things can be shown: first, if the definitions used in the argument are ambiguous, second if one or more of the propositions are wrong, or third if the logic of the argument is faulty. I've already agreed all four propositions are true, and the logic, given the propositions, is flawless. That leaves only the question of the definitions. That's where the problem lies."

"How can the definitions be the problem?"

"Well, there are two definitions that are absolutely crucial to this argument. What do we mean by 'evil' and what do we mean by 'all-powerful?'"

"Okay I'm with you so far."

"If by evil we mean that a created being was *created evil* or that evil is a *substance that was created*, then clearly that's the responsibility of the creator and then this argument would work. But what if that's not the case? Augustine, a bishop in the fourth century, wrestled with this in his *Confessions*[4] as he was struggling with the dualist teachings of Manichaeism. Manichaeism explains the problem of evil by affirming two equal and opposite uncreated powers: one good and one evil. Going back to our four propositions, the two gods are not all-powerful individually since the two of them share the power. *Augustine realized that evil was not a person or a thing, but a corruption or a twisting of something good.* So as I see it, part of the solution focuses on giving sentient, created beings free will—the ability to genuinely choose for themselves without compulsion or coercion what they'll do. The most fundamental of these decisions centers on what to do about God. Do I

---

[4] St. Augustine of Hippo. *Confessions of St. Augustine.* Translated by Edward Bouverie Pusey (Project Gutenberg; http://www.gutenberg.org/cache/epub/3296/pg3296.txt/, 2002).

want to know him and relate to him or do I want to say 'no, I'll go on without you.' That freedom is a great gift but it also contains great peril since it opens the door to choosing to reject God, and to use things for our own ends rather than for the greater good."

"I have to interrupt here, Al. I don't believe in devils. What you're saying sounds like something out of the Middle Ages."

"I know. I'm telling you the Christian position. I understand it's not consistent with your view of the world, but it does explain how Christians deal with the four propositions you raised and the problem of evil."

"But how does this get God off the hook? I thought God could always see what was going to happen. Couldn't he have made angels and people so well that they wouldn't go wrong? When we raise our kids and they turn out badly isn't at least part of the problem the parents' fault? Since God has more power, it seems to me he did a pretty shoddy job as a parent if he created 'children' that turn to evil."

"Good point Floyd. That brings me to the second definition we have to consider, "all-powerful" or "omnipotent" as the theologians call it. What does it mean? Does it mean that God can do anything at all, even if those actions disobey the law of non-contradiction?"

"What's the law of non-contradiction?"

"The law of non-contradiction states that two inherently contradictory things or events can't be true at the same time or in the same sense. Can God cause it to rain and not rain on you? The simple answer is 'no.' When he chooses to make it rain on you, he's also chosen to *not* make it *not rain*. The decision and its complement come in one package. God can make it rain on you *now* and not rain on you in 10 minutes—that's non-contradictory based on a difference in time. He can make it rain feathers and not rain water—that's non-contradictory because it's rain in a different sense.

"The imprecise definition of 'all-powerful' or 'omnipotent' is the problem. C. S. Lewis[5] talked about intrinsically impossible things (things that violate the law of non-contradiction) that are outside the definition of omnipotence. Free will is one of those things. When it's given, it

[5] C. S. Lewis. *Miracles* (New York, HarperCollins, 1996).

carries with it the possibility of evil. But true free will also means that the evil is genuinely the responsibility of the chooser. One can no longer say, 'God made me do that.'"

"Okay," said Floyd, "but God isn't only all-powerful, he's also all-knowing. Doesn't that mean he could see it coming? He would be a pretty poor chess player if he saw the difficulties and moved right into them."

"You're getting pretty close to the edge of what I can see Floyd; and what I do see, I don't see very clearly. We're confronted with a paradox. On the one hand, people are given genuine free will and free choice. I can choose to follow God or not follow him. Yet at the same time that's a gift from God and he seems to know what I will choose. How do I put those together?"

"That's exactly the contradiction I'm pointing to, Al."

"I'm a person irrevocably bound by time. Every thought and every action happens within time. But what if time is one of the things God created? Isn't that what physics is claiming now, that time is one of four dimensions like height, width and length that are inherent to our universe? As I understand it, time is different from the other three dimensions since entropy gives a direction to time. What if God is outside of time? I can't really picture it because I'm so bound by time, but what if everything to him is like the present? I seem to recall in the biblical book of Exodus when God was talking to Moses[6], he used the words 'I AM.' As I understand it, 'I AM' means *I was*, *I am*, and *I will be* all at the same time. For lack of a better analogy, what if everything is like the past, present or future all at the same time? Call it the eternal present."

"This makes no sense to me."

"Let me try another tack. Suppose you saw a movie, an accurate depiction of the Battle of Waterloo, and you saw how Napoleon might have won the battle, by launching his attack against Wellington differently."

"Assuming, I wanted Napoleon to win, which I wouldn't—okay go on."

---

[6] Exodus 3:1-22; See particularly Exodus 3:14 and the explanatory footnote in the English Standard Version (Wheaton, Good News Publishers, 2002).

"Are you responsible for Napoleon's loss simply because you had knowledge of the outcome?" asked Al.

"No, of course not. You're talking about something that happened around 200 years ago. I didn't have a chance to influence the events."

"My point is that knowing about an event isn't the same as having responsibility to influence the event. The key element in the equation is time."

"Al if I'm a parent and I see my child running onto the road and I see a car coming, won't I yell or run out to save him? Why doesn't God intervene to prevent tragedy especially for the innocent, such as children? I'm left with the conclusion that either he doesn't exist or if he does exist, he doesn't care that much."

"To be honest Floyd I struggle with this question as well. I don't really understand it, but curiously I think I know *why* I don't understand it. Your analogies (and mine) about saving children are hopeless oversimplifications for a being who—according to the teaching of the New Testament—sustains or keeps the world operating[7]. Everything that God does has implications not only for one individual, but for the whole system. He has to be just, he has to be consistent, he has to respect the free choices of parents and these parental choices do have consequences for their children because that is one of the inherent privileges of parenthood. Because I cannot even come close to imagining the complexity for the whole system, it's naïve of me to propose a tweak here and a tweak there, never realizing the global implications."

"Okay go on, I'm with you so far," said Floyd.

"But there's more. Given that I don't really understand the complexity of the world and the interactions, it's very important to me that God didn't disengage from the system."

"How do you figure that?" asked Floyd.

"It all hinges on the Jewish Carpenter. God had the courage to come and experience all of the injustices I experience. He didn't make himself exempt. Think about it. He was born apparently 'out of wedlock' in a culture that condemned that most strongly. He lived in a poor family in a backwater community that was frowned upon by the religious and

---

[7] Colossians 1:15-17.

political elite. His people were under the heel of the strongest empire that ever existed. His father likely died when Jesus was a teenager[8]. Imagine a man who healed so many yet didn't heal his own human father. Finally, he was crucified by the governing Romans at the instigation of his own people. God wrote himself into the story and didn't spare himself. At least he had the courage to face the world his creatures had made of his creation.

"This same paradox continues with his followers. Peter is rescued from death in prison because of the prayers of the church, but James is beheaded by Herod, and Stephen is stoned to death. By tradition, pretty well all of the Apostles, with the exception of John, died martyr's deaths. Why didn't God rescue them? I don't know for sure.

"So where does that leave me? I pray and am grateful for each mercy. When these tragedies come, I see them as severe mercies[9] and I trust God will make them right in the end, and perhaps someday, I will see why he said 'no!' to my prayer. That's the best I have."

"What do you mean by 'severe mercies?'" asked Floyd.

"We live in a fallen world; through our own volition the world has been warped and degraded from that which God wanted for us. So God makes the best of a bad situation by redeeming us. He begins the redemption process with the resurrection of Christ. Now he uses the hardship and tragedy as a wakeup call for his people since people often only really become attuned to their condition when hardship strikes. God does this while writing himself into this story through the incarnation, coming down to us as a human being.

Floyd looked piercingly into Al's eyes but said nothing for a while. "Okay Al," Floyd said at last, "You've presented a convoluted argument of accommodation, rationalizing the existence of evil and of God. My solution is quite simple—there is no God."

"But I think this leads to a new problem for explaining our perception of evil in the world," said Al.

"What new problem?" asked Floyd.

---

[8] We last read of Joseph at Jesus' Bar Mitzvah (Luke 2:41-52). After that we hear of Mary but not Joseph so it appears that Joseph has died in the interim.
[9] Sheldon Vanauken. *A Severe Mercy*. (New York, Harper&Row, 1977).

"By eliminating God," said Al, "we've lost the ability to explain the wrongness of the universe and of evil. There are certainly calamities. But a rational person expects those. Why do we have this innate expectation that the universe is not as it should be?

"Evil has a sense of wrongness about it, Floyd. We think it should not be. If it arises naturally in the universe, why does it repel us so much? How can you tell a line is crooked unless you have some idea of what a straight line is? I think it's hard for Naturalists to explain where this gut reaction against evil comes from. Wasn't that perception the whole power behind the apparent contradiction?"

"I don't see it," said Floyd. "Evil is just our term for the calamites that happen in a random universe, like rolling the die and landing on someone else's Boardwalk in Monopoly and going bankrupt. Crap happens."

"Using your Monopoly metaphor, we may not like landing on Boardwalk, but we recognize it's part of the game. I think our perception of evil is different than that. It's much more like playing Monopoly with a friend and learning that he's been playing with loaded dice—it's wrong. Let me get at this point another way," said Al. "Is anything wrong with anything?"

"What do you mean?"

"Is there any action at all that's wrong? Is murder wrong? Is rape wrong?"

"Of course they're wrong."

"Why are they wrong Floyd?"

"Because they hurt people and bring enormous anguish to their families. They lead to trauma and despair."

"Okay, I can see that. But why is it wrong to hurt people?" asked Al.

"I don't want to be hurt, so it's only fair not to hurt others," said Floyd.

"But don't you see? When you use the world 'fair' you're appealing to a perceived standard or unwritten rule that says 'If you don't want me to do something to you, then you shouldn't do it to me.'"

"Isn't that simply pragmatic—two people minimizing the danger to each other by choosing the pragmatic option of cooperation? After all we both benefit."

"But what if we didn't both benefit? What if you were so much stronger than me that I couldn't retaliate? Would the force of the argument dissipate? Would 'being fair' no longer be a consideration? I don't think the force of the argument would dissipate. If anything, if one party were weaker and unable to defend themselves, the unfairness would grow."

"But I try to help the weak. I wouldn't step on them if I could," protested Floyd.

"I know," said Al. "But what makes you do that?"

"I guess it wouldn't be right or fair, and I wouldn't feel good about myself if I did."

"I think what you're expressing, Floyd, is an imperative that generates an *'ought'* that tells you you ought not to oppress the weak just because you can. But where does that *'ought'* come from? As C. S. Lewis pointed out, all of the data and facts about murder and rape are in the declarative mood.[10] Yet the moral directive is in the imperative mood. No matter how often you state that murder hurts people, you can't get to 'therefore I ought not to murder' unless you're given the precept 'thou shalt not hurt people.'"

"I still don't get it," said Floyd.

"What if you think about it this way: I'm walking down the sidewalk and I see a toddler run across the street in front of a moving car. I'm faced with a split second decision. Do I run out into the road to try to save the child? If I'm just a biological machine driven by my genes to survive and reproduce, I might experience two opposing impulses. Likely the stronger one would be to choose survival and not run out to save the child. But perhaps there would also be a conflicting impulse to save the child as a way of preserving our species. If that's all there was, my decision would simply reflect the stronger of the two impulses. But I don't think that's what we mean by morality or moral choices. There would actually be a third voice in the conversation; a voice that would say I *ought* to save the child because saving the child is the right thing to do. That third voice often sides with the weaker impulse to help me do the right thing by overcoming the stronger impulse for self-preservation."

---

[10] C. S. Lewis. *The Abolition of Man.* (New York, HarperCollins, 1978) p.20.

"But Al, you've already pointed out that both saving the child and saving yourself may have advantages for the gene pool," said Floyd. "Isn't that enough to explain the decision to save the child?"

"If the central algorithm of our existence is this compulsion to pass on our genes to the next generation, then we ought to be able to analyze every action in light of that central imperative. In the example I gave you, the imperative would clearly argue to leave the child and avoid the rescue. The child is not related to me and only shares some of my genes. Furthermore, the child would be direct competition to my own children of the same sex in terms of survival, resources and reproduction. Finally I'm cutting off my own ability to produce more offspring if I sacrifice myself to save this child."

"I see that," said Floyd, "and many would choose not to rescue someone else`s child."

"But even if they did make that choice and the child died, they'd wish they'd had the courage to attempt the rescue. Floyd even you don't seem to follow that central algorithm. Why be my friend? Why help me as you do? Why do you see me as a friend rather than a competitor?"

Floyd chuckled. "A nerdy guy like you, Al, would never be competition for me on the reproductive front."

"Very funny," said Al. "Just think about what I'm saying."

"Okay, okay."

"Eliminating competition at no cost to you should be so natural that you wouldn't even think about it," continued Al. "Conversely if someone attacked you, you might not like it, but it wouldn't be wrong. In fact you would do the same if positions were reversed. So, where does evil come from? We may not have the same detailed picture of what's right and what's wrong, but everyone acts and talks as if right and wrong exist and that these are shared values. We see them most clearly when we are wronged by others. Hence the appeal when we're wronged that, 'That's not fair!'"

"Alright," said Floyd, "I get a glimmer of what you're driving at. If right and wrong—or morality if you like—is something I make up for myself, then why do I have this expectation that other people should follow my made up rules? It's like dressing a certain way or preferring one kind of music over another. It would be unreasonable to expect others to automatically like and choose my choices. I'll have to think about it. It may still be a biological necessity that's essential for our cooperation."

Floyd pushed back from the table, his face clouding over. "Why are we talking about these hypothetical situations? My grandmother died and I love her. Why do I feel this terrible emptiness when I think of her?"

Floyd looked Al straight in the eye. "I feel this pain for reasons I don't understand, and you're giving me these platitudes about a God who loves me. And yet I live in this universe full of crap. We're friends, but I find it offensive that you would believe in this God who's supposed to be good, but he takes my grandmother and leaves me with this colossal desolation. Someday he's going to do the same to me. And to my wife and children, if they should ever come along. I'm sick of the thought of this God who leaves us in this state! I guess I believe in God just enough to hate him!"

Floyd scowled and jumped to his feet, knocking his chair and the tray of dishes clattering to the floor.

"Floyd, you're being irrational! That's the weight of my argument. The emotion proves my point."

Floyd picked up his tray and dishes, placed them back down on the table, righted his chair and sat down heavily. He ran his hand over his shaven head and sat staring at his tray.

Al could feel the eyes of everyone in the cafeteria looking at them. He took off his glasses and rubbed his eyes. *What a fool I am. Here I am prating on about respectful conversation and I talk like this.*

The silence grew uncomfortable. "I'm sorry Floyd. Calling you 'irrational' was an insult which I said I wouldn't do."

Floyd looked up and a faint smile crossed his face. "We *were* going to keep this conversation civil," he said gently and then his smile broadened. "Well, calling me irrational, that's a first for you; I guess I gotcha going. But seriously, we have a lot to think about. We should head off to class. Let's think about what we said. It looks like it's gonna be a beautiful day. How about we go fishing after class? That should calm us down."

"Fishing," said Al. "Great idea!"

FOUR

Two Kinds of Questions

That evening Al dug out his fishing gear, donned his hat festooned with fishing flies, and waited for Floyd by the library. He was just beginning to think Floyd had been detained when he saw him coming around the corner of the library, dressed in khakis and carrying a brand new fishing rod and reel.

"What do you think?" asked Floyd brandishing the new rod.

Al took the rod Floyd offered and whipped the tip up and down. "Great action. I love the open face reel. What brought this on?"

"Oh I figured I was due. I wouldn't be caught dead with the fish-meister carrying my old equipment."

Al laughed, "Yes, you could have. Men really only need the tiniest of reasons to buy new fishing gear."

"Okay, okay." said Floyd. "Where are we heading today?"

"I thought we'd head to the north side of the island." Al led the way off the main campus grounds and headed into the heavily wooded hills, picking their way up an indistinct path that looked more like a game track than a hiking trail.

"Are you taking me to your secret fishing spot, Al?"

"I am. It's the best place on the island to catch sea bass."

That morning's confrontation had been eating at Al all day. "Floyd, I'm sorry I lost my temper this morning. It's bothered me all day. I thought I was immune to getting heated about this discussion. I've found out I'm not."

"No problem, Al. You don't show enough emotion. Must be all that 'turn the other cheek' indoctrination. But, I've seen some Christians absolutely lose it. Tends to be those who have such a strong sense they're right that any question or disagreement is seen as an attack. And man can they fight back."

"I know what you mean, Floyd. Unfortunately Christians often have the same reaction—even with each other—when they disagree about doctrine."

"I've seen that too. If they're supposedly on the same team why do they disagree with each other?" asked Floyd.

"Well for one reason, we're talking about very important questions," said Al, "and when we begin to doubt the answers we think we've found, those doubts can really rock our world."

"I suppose you're right, Al. Now that you mention it, Atheists like me aren't immune to having our world shaken up when our worldviews are questioned either, but in the end shouldn't we be searching for the truth, no matter how much mental anguish the search causes? After all, aren't we just destroying illusions?"

"I couldn't agree with you more Floyd. Still, I have to work to keep that attitude foremost in my mind."

"Let me go back to what you said earlier, Al. I'm mightily puzzled that you said you 'questioned your way to faith.' After all didn't Jesus react negatively to questions? I seem to recall that from my Vacation Bible School training. See, I was paying attention. If he reacted negatively to questions, doesn't that indicate Christians as a group would be predisposed the same way?"

"Let me think about that," said Al.

In silence, Al and Floyd emerged from the woods and crested a hill. The coast of North Carolina stretched out below them. They followed the path back into the woods and down the other side of the hill. They moved so quietly, Al could hear a rivulet flowing in the woods off to his left. He led them toward the sound. "We should cross over the creek here," said Al. They crossed the small creek by leaping from rock to rock. Al searched for a path on the other side.

"Here it is." The path was barely perceptible, but Al knew this terrain well. Soon they emerged on a granite shelf with the waves breaking on the rock at their feet. They unloaded their gear, baited their hooks and cast them into the surf.

Al settled down comfortably. The beauty of the place filled him with tranquility. He could see small islands ahead of them. Further to the west, the bridge from the island met the mainland, and the pavement—like a black snake—disappeared into the wooded hills. Gulls circled overhead. Small white clouds dotted the sky.

"Where were we?" asked Al.

"I was asking about Jesus' reaction to questions," said Floyd. "I was making the point that since he reacted negatively to questions, he was teaching his followers to have the same attitude."

"When I was reading Luke's account of Jesus' life recently," Al said, "there was a short description of Jesus as a boy sitting at the Rabbis' feet listening and asking questions in the temple in Jerusalem.[11] As Christians we believe that Jesus is actually the Creator come as a human being, so it's astounding to me that he would listen and ask questions. But I think he's shown that honest questions—where one asks a question and listens to the answer because one is genuinely interested in gaining knowledge—are always welcomed by him. I believe that's why he modeled that questioning behavior."

"But didn't Jesus also react negatively to questions, Al?"

"Yes he did. So how do I reconcile those reactions? It seems to me there are two kinds of questions. Some questions are honest questions where the questioner is asking to be enlightened, and listens to the answer. But there is a second kind of question where the question is really a trap, a criticism, or censure in question form. In one sense these are not questions at all, but simply a clever way of calling the other person's argument or statement *into question*."

"Sort of like when I used to get home late," said Floyd, "and my mother would ask me 'Where have you been?' She wasn't just asking for information. She suspected I'd been getting into trouble and would keep grilling me until she was satisfied with my answer."

---

[11] Luke 2:46

"I didn't realize you were that kind of a teenager," said Al. "A lot about you is beginning to make sense to me now."

"Stop it and get back to your train of thought."

"Okay," said Al grinning. "Jesus often faced this second kind of question, especially from the religious leaders of his day. If you read Jesus' biographies carefully you realize the questioners were often not interested in the answer at all, but only in getting Jesus into difficulty with the authorities. You may remember when he was asked whether or not the Jewish people should pay taxes to the Romans[12]. This question was a trap since a 'no' would bring Jesus into trouble with the Romans. On the other hand a 'yes' would alienate the Jewish people since they deeply resented paying taxes to their oppressors. Jesus answered their trap with another question: 'Whose image do you see on the coin?'[13] The key point of the second kind of question is that the questioner is not so much interested in learning from the answer as in putting the responder into difficulty. This kind of question is inherently unfriendly and antagonistic. Sort of like many of the questions asked in Congress."

"Sort of like my mother putting me into a difficult corner when she cross-examined me about my lateness," said Floyd.

"I suppose, but in your case her questions were undoubtedly justified."

"You sound as if you've been talking to my mother, Al."

"Well, no I haven't," said Al.

"That's a relief. If she said something, I'd never hear the end of it. So where was this conversation going when we became sidetracked with my mother's questions?"

"We were talking about two kinds of questions," said Al. "Your mother's questions were of the second sort. Rather than just seeking information about what you were doing, her question 'where have you been?' was a challenge for you to prove that you were behaving yourself even though you arrived home very late. The motive is completely different from those who ask questions genuinely looking for answers.

---

[12] Matthew 22:15-22
[13] Matthew 22:20-21

"And, when you think about it, there are two kinds of people who never ask *the first kind of question*: those who don't believe in answers (or aren't willing to believe the answers) and those who have all the answers. But these people may still ask the incriminating question—aiming to discredit their opponents. Many of our contemporaries fall into this second category. When they talk to religious people they ask questions to cast the religious people in a foolish light. But in their hearts they don't really listen to the answers because it's just an intellectual game in a world that—to them—has no real answers. Or else their concept of the world refuses to include religious answers in the real answer category. It's hard having a significant conversation with people who only care about putting you into difficulty and don't care about the answers at all."

"So what has that to do with Jesus responding negatively to questions?" asked Floyd.

"Jesus met both categories of these questioners, neither of whom cared about his answers except for the hope of discrediting him. One group—the Sadducees—were very politically minded and thought many of the questions of their day had no answers. The other group— the Pharisees—believed they had all the answers. Surprisingly, even though these groups were—in many ways—polar opposites, the kinds of questions the Pharisees asked Jesus were very similar to the questions the Sadducees asked him. They were designed to trap Jesus into speaking sedition by criticizing the Romans, or to show that he was ignorant and uneducated. Those were all traps and cheats disguised as questions and that's why Jesus reacted negatively. Whenever he encountered a person who genuinely wanted to know answers, Jesus responded quite differently."

"Well I have to admit, until this business with Grandma, I was in the Sadducee camp. I thought Christians were fools chasing a pipedream. I only asked questions to show them they were wrong."

"Has that changed?"

"Well, I'm not saying that you've moved me an inch toward your position, but I can learn some things from you."

"I feel the same. As a Christian, I'm faced with two terrible consequences of my religiosity. One is to become so convinced I'm right, that like the Pharisees, I stop listening to people and only focus on convincing them to think as I do as a way of converting them."

"What's the second?"

"Patrick O'Brian in his Aubrey-Maturin seafaring novels wrote about the terrible burden of moral superiority. As a Christian I try to do the right thing and live by high standards. Inevitably one develops this mindset of moral superiority. It destroys my ability to relate to people and leads to pride—the greatest sin of all. I honestly don't know how to simultaneously strive to do the right thing while being totally unconscious of the effort. Yet that's the conundrum we all face as we try to live a more moral life."

"I'll keep you on track Al. If you get self-righteous and uppity, I'll put you back in your proper place."

"I'm sure I won't like it. I'd be upset if one of my friends pointed out the defects that everyone sees anyway. He wouldn't receive the thanks the information deserved, so I'll thank you in advance Floyd for setting me straight."

"I'm always glad to upbraid you, Al."

"Speaking about the evil of self-righteousness and pride in the Christian sphere reminds me of something I wanted to talk about," said Al. "Remember when we talked about the four propositions relating to the problem of evil?"

"Yeah, I remember."

"We talked about how Atheists deny the existence of God and so they're simply left with the proposition that evil exists."

"I'm with you."

"This brings me to one of the cardinal difficulties of atheism—where does morality come from?"

"Why is that a difficulty? I think morality comes from our conditioning towards cooperation. Since the earliest days of our species, we've survived by cooperation. So we appear moral or fair-minded when we're actually looking after ourselves. After all, people who are reprobates and selfish almost never get a break, help, or goodwill. In the long run being a "nice guy" actually works. Morality is essentially pragmatic."

"So morality is mere pragmatism," said Al. "Let me try that out. Let's say your car breaks down at the side of the road, and a man stops to offer assistance. It turns out he's a mechanic and spends quite some time fixing your car without asking for any compensation. How would you react?"

"I'd think he's a very generous guy who likes to help others. I'd probably think of the times I drove past someone who needed help and I didn't stop."

"I would think the same. Now what if right after he stopped, another vehicle from the local television station stopped by and filmed him fixing your car? You realize he's a politician and he's using this circumstance to bolster his chances of winning an election. How would that change your view of him?"

"I'd be grateful I was lucky enough he fixed my car while he was pulling his publicity stunt."

"Would you feel used?"

"Yeah, I guess I'd feel used. In the first case he did it just to help me. I'd feel like he cared about me—in some way—and about my situation. With the second I'd feel like a stepping stone in his career. I'd suspect that what mattered most to him was getting the film footage and being able to say he'd helped someone."

"Of course," agreed Al. "C. S. Lewis is a writer who's impressed me a great deal. He once compared morality to a fleet of ships.[14] One thing every fleet of ships has to accomplish is to avoid colliding with one another. That's the kind of pragmatic morality you're talking about, Floyd, 'I won't hurt you if you won't hurt me.' That's the morality that almost everyone talks about. But there are two other kinds, or levels, of morality. The first has to do with the ships themselves. The captain has to keep his own ship in good operating condition. If the engine breaks down or the rudder rusts through, then despite his best intentions at avoiding collisions, the captain may not be able to do so because of the sorry state of his ship. That means I have a responsibility to 'be good' even when no one is watching."

---

[14] C. S. Lewis, *Mere Christianity* (New York, Simon & Schuster, 1980) p.70-71.

"I can see that," said Floyd.

"But there's a third kind of morality," continued Al. "Why have the ships put to sea in the first place? Where are they going and what are they meant to accomplish? Even if the ships are in excellent condition, and sail in perfect formation yet end up in Australia when they were sent to the Mediterranean, then they've failed. Morality can only have a purpose or mission if the universe has a purpose. Theism gives a point to morality that atheism can never give it."

"But why does morality have to have a purpose?" asked Floyd. "Can't it just exist?"

"Doesn't purpose always supersede aimlessness?" asked Al. "If you were a sailor sailing in this fleet in the middle of the Atlantic, maintaining your ship and avoiding collisions, wouldn't you ask 'why are we here rather than somewhere else?'"

"I suppose," said Floyd.

"And if someone were to discover lost orders—that you were supposed to deliver your cargo to famine victims in Cameroon—wouldn't that transform a mindless and pointless exercise into something vital?"

"I can see that."

"So it seems to me that purpose always transcends aimlessness."

"Okay, I'll put a check mark next to that answer. Purpose does add value," said Floyd. "You talked about atheism's problems with morality. But theism also has a major problem. You've been arguing that God is needed for morality. But how does God do that? Does he give us the moral laws by fiat or is he also under the law? As Bertrand Russell points out, this dichotomy leads to a contradiction. If God makes up the laws to please himself, how is he different from any tyrant who makes up his own invented laws and then uses his power to compel others to follow his dictates? Won't the purpose you just alluded to in the end just be God's capriciousness? On the other hand, if the moral law is above God, how can he be all-powerful?"

"As a Theist," said Al, "I would affirm both at the same time."

"Why am I *not* surprised?"

"God's morality arises out of his nature," continued Al. "It's neither something he invents and then commands for others, nor is it above him, in the sense that he has to obey morality as we do. In other words God is not dependent on another source for his morality.

"I thought God never lied or was unjust. That sounds like compulsion to me," said Floyd.

"Floyd, think of it this way. If you're an honorable man and have a strong conviction that you won't deceive, does that mean you can't make your mouth and tongue form the words of a lie? No it means that even though you have the muscle control to lie, and the intelligence to formulate a deception, your moral character prevents those things from happening. God could lie in the same sense: he has the power to form the deception, but his character prevents him from exercising that power."

"So where does this discussion leave us?" asked Floyd.

"Steven Weinberg[15] is one of the more thoughtful Atheists I've read who takes up this position. In his book *Facing Up*, he affirms that people make up their own morality. But then, he answers any statement that in atheism there is no basis for morality with the rejoinder that, 'I and other Atheists are as moral or more moral than most Christians.'"

"What's wrong with that? It's true!" said Floyd.

"It may well be true, but think about what that means. If morality is something I make up or invent, then it's like making up and marking my own test. Since I'm making the whole thing up and also judging my own answers, of course I'll get whatever grade I want to give myself."

"Again, I ask, 'What's wrong with that?'" asked Floyd.

"If you take that position, you have no objective basis for telling anyone their actions are wrong. You ought to say to everyone else, 'of course what you do is perfectly consistent with your morality since you made it up and might change it tomorrow.'"

"Okay Al. I follow you."

"What if someone decides that being an axe murderer is consistent with his morality?" asked Al.

"We lock him up or maybe execute him," said Floyd. "I don't have to be a Christian to have laws that protect society."

---

[15] Steven Weinberg, *Facing Up. Science and Its Cultural Adversaries* (Boston: Harvard University Press, 2003).

"But what's happened is that *power* has become a substitute for *morality* or *right*."

"How so?" asked Floyd.

"At the trial, if the defendant asks 'Why can't I keep beheading people?' your answer has to be, 'Because we say so.' You can no longer say 'Because it's wrong.'"

"Doesn't that work?" asked Floyd.

"I suppose it works, but you've left the world of morality."

"Why?"

"Morality appeals to a common standard," said Al. "There can be no common standard if morality is individual and invented. Morality comes with an *ought*. I may not follow moral principles but there's a part of me that recognizes I *ought* to do some things, such as that mechanic stopping to help someone in need."

Al felt a bite on his line. He gave a quick tug to set the hook and then gave the fish a bit of line. After minutes of pulling the line taut, reeling in the slack, Floyd scooped up a three pound sea bass in their net, and held it up for Al to see his catch. It was a fine specimen.

When Floyd cast his line, he immediately had a bite. And so followed one of those glorious fishing experiences, in which nearly every cast produced a fish.

"Aren't you going to tell me that you've prayed for our fishing and this is a demonstration of God's existence?" asked Floyd mischievously.

"No Floyd, I think this most definitely is an act of grace.

FIVE

The Problem of Evil Committed by Christians

"You hungry?" Al asked dangling the fat sea bass from his rod.

"You clean the fish," Floyd said, "I'll get the fire started."

"Sure thing; sea bass always tastes best when it's fresh."

Floyd nodded and headed to a sheltered dell beneath a rocky ridge to a small fire pit.

They had only kept the largest of the sea bass. Al began cleaning the fish. He heard twigs snapping.

Floyd reappeared. "Do you have any matches?"

"In the second drawer of my tackle box." Al deftly gutted the big sea bass and cut four generous fillets. He buried the head and entrails and carried the four fillets in the frying pan into the dell. Floyd had a small fire going.

Al set the skillet down and unpacked a small grill from his knapsack, placing it between two rocks.

"You've obviously done this before," said Floyd.

"This is one of my favorite things!" Al pulled out the small lunch cooler and produced a package of potato salad from the cafeteria."

"What would you like to drink, Floyd?"

"What do you have?"

"My favorite wheat beer from Benson's Microbrewery or cola?

"I'll take the beer."

Al flipped the fillets with his hunting knife and a freshly cut stick. He added salt and looked critically at the fillets. "I think they're done."

"Good. I'm starving."

"Can you get the two plates out of my knapsack, Floyd?"

"Sure. Boy I don't normally like fish but that smells great."

"There's something special about fresh fish. Here, help yourself to the potato salad."

They ate in silence. After dinner Al rinsed off their plates and the frying pan in the sea. When he returned to the dell, Floyd was nursing his beer and leaning back against a fallen log, looking up at the sky. "This is the life Al."

"I couldn't agree more, Floyd." Al watched the evening sun tinge the sea orange.

The beauty of the sea and the sky is a meal on its own.

Floyd was silent for a while. Al looked at him. His friend seemed to be thinking.

Floyd cleared his throat. "Al, back to our previous discussion, your argument about God being good simply doesn't add up. How many wars have been fought over religion? I remember reading about the Thirty Years' War, that Christian religious war between Catholics and Protestants. About two thirds of the population of what is now Germany was killed. The Philippines were converted to Catholicism from Islam by the sword, all except one island, which the Spanish couldn't easily land on in force. Look how Christians have treated the Jews. How can God be the moral force you make him out to be if so much evil is done by his followers in his name? Your argument would be much more convincing if Christians were actually a force for good rather than evil."

"Floyd, in a great many ways you're right. Much evil has been done in the name of Christianity. In fact G. K. Chesterton and others as I recall, made the point that the best argument against Christianity is Christians.

"Still I don't think the argument against Christianity on this ground is as strong as you make it," continued Al. "First of all, if you look at nations and peoples before the French Revolution, every one of them was religious. Therefore it's easy to look at a multidimensional problem and say they committed evil because of religion. What about politics? What about greed? What about power? Didn't these play a role?"

"I'm sure they did. But the Thirty Years' War was ostensibly a religious war wasn't it?" asked Floyd.

"That's exactly my point," said Al. We pick from a host of causes and label it a 'religious war' when we could just as easily call it a war for political power and control. Have we stopped fighting just because we're less religious?"

"I suppose not," conceded Floyd.

"We haven't," said Al. "If we focus on governments that are *openly antagonistic* to religion, have they done any better? The French Revolution—after proclaiming the noble sentiments of equality, fraternity, and freedom—moved quickly on to the Reign of Terror, and then on to Napoleon's long war to dominate Europe.

"Have the Communists done better? They're avowedly atheistic and have killed a great many people in the pogroms and mass exterminations of dissenters. I think the root problem is not really religion, but a *lack of respect for Freedom of Religion.* If we respected the rights of people to make up their own minds without coercion, then we wouldn't do these things. But all governments prefer a homogeneous populace. So there's a tendency to make us all the same because then we're easier to manage and govern. Coercion can just as easily be secular as religious."

"How do those excesses excuse the Christians?" asked Floyd.

"They don't, but I think people who raise this issue are overlooking an important fact."

"What's that?" asked Floyd.

"If you're a power hungry tyrant, and you want your followers to join in a cause that's dear to your heart, it will never do to say 'Let's beat up on our neighbors. I know they pose no threat. They haven't done us a stitch of harm, but let's kill them, take their land, and enslave them. Come on—it'll be fun.'"

"Go on."

"The vast majority of people are too fair minded to risk their own lives, and the lives of their children on such an escapade. But if the war monger builds a case that the neighbor poses a threat and will attack us, take our freedom, our children and our lands, then the call to war becomes much more credible. The appeal to religion has worked for tyrants *because religion was so valuable to the people.* It gave meaning to their lives. And so by having that threatened, one could twist their sense of right and wrong to commit atrocities because in their fear they succumbed to the argument that the end justified the means. Today with the decline of religion in the West, we make the same calls using our new values. Now the threat is that others will impose their unwanted religion on us, take away our wealth, our children and our freedoms. Aren't we hearing the need for 'shared values?' Don't we fight wars for democracy? Don't we impose our will on others claiming that we're defending individual freedoms? These are good causes, but they can become reasons for bloodshed and tyranny. The same story works. The same people are pulling the strings. Since religion is not seen as being as valuable as it once was, it's no longer used as much to justify aggression. But other things are."

"Still that doesn't excuse them," said Floyd.

"No not at all. If you follow the teachings of Jesus, *the end never justifies the means.* That's a great trap. What makes things worse is that our evil nature always makes it seem as if the injustices foisted on us are grievous beyond words. And yet when we do the very same thing to someone else, it's a justifiable necessity on our part. We are hopelessly unsymmetrical in our evaluations."

"Still why do they fall for it?" asked Floyd.

"We're fallen creatures. We're under repair so we're not there yet. The New Testament teaches us to regard others—even those who think differently from us—as brothers. We're to return good for evil and love our enemies. The end never justifies the means—yet Christians still can be moved to do things that go against their fundamental teachings. Why do they do it? Why do I do it? I'm far from perfect, and so are they, I guess."

Al ran his hand over his forehead and began remembering all the things he had done wrong. It began to wash over him like a flood. *Why do I do those things? Why is theory so clear cut and practice so difficult?*

He looked up at Floyd. "When I look at myself, even though I've been a Christian for a while, I still regularly come to points where I have to say to Christ, the person I've committed to following, 'Forgive me, I really blew it. Help me do better.' So why does that happen? I've been redeemed in the sense that I'm under new management and I've given ownership over to Christ. But I still have free will. And I still have old habits and a part of me that still wants to live for myself. I think I lie to myself a lot and mislead myself.

"Even when I'm lucid, and I'm not blinded by self-deception, decisions are not always easy. C. S. Lewis once said, 'Never mistake a necessary evil for a good.' I think he was right. We and God, I suppose, given the actions of free will are sometimes faced with alternatives, none of which is good, and none of which we would've chosen if the circumstances had dealt us a better hand. Reporting your child for drug use, violently intervening in a fight, or a country undertaking military action to stave off a massacre, are examples that come to mind."

"Well, I would do the same. But I meant actions that are clearly evil," said Floyd.

"But if I haven't walked in those people's shoes and seen the decision-making process through their eyes, maybe I'm simply an armchair quarterback chiding a player who's being hammered by a defensive lineman for a bad throw. I haven't walked in their shoes. I haven't faced the pressures they faced as they made their decision. Perhaps if the decision happened many years ago, I now have the benefit of seeing clearly that they were wrong about many of their assumptions. But at the time they didn't know that."

"Al, I hear what you're saying and I concede that when people criticize my own decisions they often don't understand either the pressure of the moment or the perspective I had when I made my decision. I often think they'd be more charitable if they spent more time walking in my shoes than criticizing me. But on the other hand, when I look at Christians through the ages: the Crusades, Bartholomew's Day Massacre, and the Inquisition, it's hard to make excuses for those events."

"Floyd, of the examples cited, Christians weren't only the perpetrators, but also the victims. Even in the Crusades, if I remember my history, the rabble army caused great damage to Byzantium, the people they were supposed to be helping, and in the sack of Jerusalem, Muslims, Christians and Jews who made up the population of Jerusalem were all put to the sword. Part of the difficulty is that you use the word Christians in your description. I think you and I could agree on this question a good deal more if you substituted "religion" for "God" and "Christians."

"Al, I don't see how that will help you. Isn't Christianity a religion?"

"That depends on the definition. If you think of religion as the institutions, the laws, the regulations that are supposed to bring us close to God, then Christianity, as far as I can tell from reading the New Testament, was never meant to be a religion. Indeed, in the Gospels, Jesus' strongest words of censure were directed toward the Pharisees, the religious heavyweights of his day, and he accused them of keeping people who were truly seeking God away from God by loading them down with regulations, duties, and obligations which were the constructs of men and not of God. Christianity is much more about meeting a person, than following a program."

"Okay you're trying to draw a distinction between Christianity and religions. I've heard that before," said Floyd.

"Floyd, getting back to the question about 'religion being the root of all evil…'"

"I never said *all* evil, but I believe Christians are responsible for much of the evil in our world."

"Let me turn this discussion on its head. I can see why the behavior by Christians, or as I prefer, 'religious people' should bother me since I see clearly how they don't conform to the behavior God has set out for Christians. *But why does it bother you?* At the risk of being repetitive, if all people, including Christians, are the product of millions of years of evolution, through which we've been conditioned by our genes to eliminate competition and reproduce as prolifically as possible, then wouldn't we expect the killing off of competition to be the most natural of activities? Would rape and pillaging not be entirely consistent with that conditioning? At their worst are these "Christians" from the Thirty Years' War not acting exactly as one would have predicted based on evolution. So why the surprise? Why the expectation that they'd be better?

"It seems to me the anomaly—from your point of view—would be those people who rise above this 'ethic' of me and mine first."

"So you're saying," said Floyd, "that my baseline for behavior should be the behavior of a predator and so I should be accepting the bad behavior as normal rather than condemning it? I see your point, but there's this attitude in me that very much wants to condemn this. So why do I feel that way? I don't really know."

"As always," said Al smiling, "you're better than your principles and that's why you're such a good friend."

Floyd had that perplexed look of a man trying to determine if the last statement worked out to a compliment. "You have a point," he said, shaking himself and looking around. "I'm cold and it's getting dark. We should be heading back. Will you put out the fire while I collect up our gear?"

SIX

The Problem of Physical Calamity

The next Saturday dawned, promising a spectacular day. Al went outside to the little park near his residence, Socrates, to read his Bible. The air was fresh and warm even this early in the morning. He watched a honeybee pollinating clover and thought about his reading. The Gospel of John, Chapter 13 tells of Jesus washing the Disciples' feet after their Passover meal, just before he was taken into custody as a prelude to his crucifixion.

Lord, why did you do that? I know you're telling me to serve my brothers and sisters. There's so much wrapped up in that simple act. When you are washing a person's dirty feet, you can't do so without picking up some of the dirt yourself. When the Master chose to do a servant's job, none of the Disciples could ever feel above the task.

There's so much in that act. Lord you often seem to speak to me by bringing these thoughts to my mind when I let you.

"I thought I might find you here."

Al looked up to see Floyd standing there in his jeans. "Floyd, you're up early. Are you enjoying this glorious morning?"

"I'll enjoy it more when we go on our hike."

"Our hike?"

"Gleeson, you can't spend this beautiful Saturday reading books. We need to get out. Let's hike to the top of South Mountain, I bet we'll see for miles."

"Alright, give me time to get my things together."

Three hours later they reached the south-facing lookout on South Mountain. The ledge at about 1800 feet gave them a wonderful view of the ocean and the North Carolina coastline to the south. Off to their left, the roof of the nuclear power plant that ran the electrical grid for the university and served as a training platform in nuclear physics, peeked above the trees. Farther left, the naval station stood nestled in a small bay with three patrol boats in dock. Al had forgotten the station was there. The navy fellows kept to themselves and the facility was off limits to students.

Floyd handed Al a sandwich and a bottle of beer. "Ready to continue our discussions?"

"Of course."

Floyd took a deep breath. "Your whole argument so far has focused on evil caused by people making decisions that hurt others. In other words it's not God's fault but people's free will. But what about natural disasters; people dying of disease, earthquakes, famine, volcanic eruptions, and tsunamis? Wouldn't you say those are the direct actions of God? Your free will argument won't work in this case."

"No, free will wouldn't work directly although it may still play indirectly," said Al. "We seem to be in a world that's not quite right. A world that has things in it that we both feel shouldn't be as they are."

"So why would this good, all-powerful, all-knowing God do that?"

"From my study of the scriptures, I don't have a good answer. I know the world isn't as it should be, but I don't clearly see how natural disasters fit in. On the one hand they're part of what makes this world what it is. You and I both know that tsunamis and earthquakes arise out of plate tectonics, which give us many of the features such as this mountain we love so much. I was reading recently about some speculations on the geology of Venus. Some planetary geologists[16] believe Venus undergoes a plugged pressure cooker effect where the pressure of subterranean heat builds up to such an extent that eventually there are lava flows that pretty

---

[16] D.L. Bindschadler (1995). "Magellan: A new view of Venus' geology and geophysics". *American Geophysical Union*, as cited by http://en.wikipedia.org/wiki/Volcanology_of_Venus/.

well cover the whole planet. So, terrible as they are, plate tectonics and the earthquakes they engender, may be a safety valve for us to prevent an even bigger disaster.

"Hurricanes and thunderstorms are part of the weather of this world. It seems as if the world, in a macroscopic sense, has the same problem we have individually. Just as we're individually out of control, so these forces, although they have a beneficial role to play, seem to be out of control, as if we're children in a factory where the owner and workers have left or been driven out."

"Okay, but what would it look like if it were fixed?" asked Floyd.

"Maybe they'd be a necessary part of the world that God intended, but we'd know when these disasters were coming. Or perhaps if we saw more clearly and concretely that physical death is not the end of things, and we had an open, intimate relationship with God, then we wouldn't take these calamities so severely."

"Go on," said Floyd.

"You see I have a problem with how some people imagine the next life," continued Al. "They imagine the idyllic life is like a nursery school room where all dangers have been removed. That seems to me to be insipid and boring. We need some danger and excitement, but not too much. In C. S. Lewis' novel *Out of the Silent Planet*[17], the inhabitants of Mars hunted a predatory fish called Hnakra. Although the Hnakra often killed the inhabitants, the Hnakra hunt was what added zest and excitement to their lives. In that book, Mars didn't need to be fixed like the Silent Planet, Earth, which was under the control of warped super beings. Still Mars had its dangers. Indeed the danger is what added to the spice of life for the inhabitants. Perhaps if our world and the people in it were not so twisted and broken, we'd feel the same."

"It sounds an awful lot to me as if you're trying to justify these calamities," said Floyd. "Why not recognize them for the terrible tragedy they are and be done with it? As an Atheist I can do that."

"But don't you see, Floyd, that we run into the same problem we encountered before?"

"How so?"

---

[17] C. S. Lewis, *Out of the Silent Planet* (London, Pan Books, 1938), p. 86.

"Well if I'm a product of this world," said Al, "if I've arisen in it through millions of years of evolutionary change with microscopic mutations accumulating over time to fit me for this world, *why am I in such reaction against it?* Earthquakes, tsunamis, and thunderstorms should be the most natural thing in the world."

"Even animals are afraid of thunderstorms," said Floyd.

"Being afraid is one thing, but I think we're talking about more—we have a sense that it shouldn't be like this. We don't accept the loss of life due to earthquakes. We see it as unnatural and offensive. I don't sense that in animals. They may be afraid or angry, but they seem at home in it in a way we're not. We think the world is wrong."

"I'm getting hot," said Floyd. "Let's climb down to the lake and take a swim."

The climb down from the ledge proved hot work. When Al and Floyd finally reached the bottom they walked through the pine forest to the edge of the Upper Lake.

"Isn't this pumped storage system an amazing feat of engineering, Floyd?"

"You mean using the Upper and Lower Lakes as a source of hydroelectric power?"

"Yes. They allow the nuclear plant to run at constant load. The hydro-electric plant can handle the peak loads. When loads are low, the nuclear power can shift to refilling the Upper Lake through the pumping station.

"What's particularly clever is that the same turbine can be used as a pump or a generator, simply by reversing the direction of rotation. I think it's called a Pelton Turbine."

"Ingenious. But we don't want to swim near the pipes. Where are they Al?"

"The pipes are over at the other side of the lake. We're safe here."

They were sitting on a rock that jutted out into the lake. The water was quite deep beyond the rock.

"Let me see your wallet, Al?"

"Why?"

"I've heard you can tell a lot about a person from the contents of their wallet," said Floyd.

What a strange request. Al took his wallet out of his pocket and handed it to Floyd. Floyd opened the wallet up and pulled out Al's student ID and driver's license.

"Floyd, be careful. You're close to the water's edge. Don't drop them in the water."

"Relax Gleeson." Floyd pulled out a little card. "What's this?"

Al leaned over and looked at the card. "That's my periodic table."

"You keep a periodic table in your wallet?"

"Of course. Don't you have a periodic table in your wallet?" asked Al in mock surprise.

"Of course not. You're supposed to have a picture of your girlfriend."

"I don't have a girlfriend."

"Of course you don't," said Floyd. "Anyone who keeps a periodic table in their wallet isn't likely to have a girlfriend."

"Ouch," said Al with a grin. "I'm deeply wounded."

"Yeah, right."

"Besides, I do have pictures in my wallet. Let me show you," said Al.

Floyd playfully held the wallet just out of reach so Al had to stretch for it. Feeling a solid push on his back, Al's arms flailed momentarily as he tried to right himself. Hopelessly over balanced, he had the good sense to close his mouth before hitting the water. It was so cold the shock took his breath away. With water up his nose, Al sputtered.

Floyd guffawed on shore. "Al, you're so trusting and gullible."

"I guess I am. Are you coming in? I'd try to pull you in, but I'm sure you're expecting that."

"Oh yeah, I am." Floyd took off his shirt, stripped down to his bathing suit, then ran the length of the rock and cannon balled into the water. Al turned his head but received another nose full of water.

Al climbed out of the water, retrieved his small pack and changed into his bathing suit. Arranging his clothes on the rock to dry in the sun, he dove back into the water. The bracing cold water seemed warmer after Al's body adjusted to it. Floyd, who had been floating lazily, pointed to a tiny rock protruding from the water about 100 meters distant and began to slowly swim towards it. When Al caught up, Floyd picked up his pace. Even swimming as fast as he could, Al couldn't keep up with Floyd. When the two finally reached the rock, they turned around and lazily swam the backstroke to shore.

"Isn't this the life?" asked Floyd between strokes.

"I couldn't agree more."

They climbed out of the water and dried off in the sun.

"I was talking to a guy I know, called Stan Bigelow about our conversation," said Floyd. "His immediate reaction was, 'Okay who created God? How did he get here?'"

"Who created God?" asked Al. "I think one of the key points about God is that he has to be *outside the realm of cause and effect*. He has to be the 'uncaused causer.'"

"I don't see it," said Floyd.

"It's one of the arguments for the existence of God; it's called the Kalam argument. If you read Kreeft and Tacelli's book, *Christian Apologetics*, they list 23 arguments for the existence of God.[18] The Kalam argument is one of them.[19]"

"So what's this Kalam Argument?" asked Floyd.

"It essentially says that in a cause and effect universe you can't have an infinite regression of causes."

"Why not?"

"I'm not a philosopher, but I've explained the Kalam argument to myself this way: suppose I told you that I'd sent you a letter, but the post office told me it would have to pass through an infinite number of hands before it reaches you. When would you receive my letter?"

"Since each hand-off takes a finite amount of time," mused Floyd, "I'd never get your letter because the travel time is infinite."

"Exactly. We're here in this point of time at the end of a long series of causes that give rise to effects, which in turn are new causes that give rise to new effects. It's easy to see that if I sent you a letter that passed

[18] Peter Kreeft and Ronald K. Tacelli, *Handbook of Christian Apologetics* (Downers Grove, IVP Academic, 1994), p. 48-88.

[19] Peter Kreeft and Ronald K. Tacelli, *Handbook of Christian Apologetics* (Downers Grove, IVP Academic, 1994), p. 58-60.

through an infinite number of hands, you'd never get it. But the same problem that's easy to see going forward also exists going backward. If there is no uncaused cause, and you trace the cause and effect sequence backward infinitely as your question, 'who created God suggests,' all reason for our existence vanishes. Everything that exists is like that letter that can't arrive. We shouldn't be here if the first cause is displaced infinitely into the past."

"But I can trace the cause and effect sequence backward."

"Each of those is like the post office letter hand-off. We're talking about the start when the letter was sent."

Floyd scratched his head. "What about mathematics? Can't I define an infinite series going backward?"

"Let me think about that," said Al. He rolled onto his stomach and stared across the lake. "How do I bring cause and effect into your mathematical metaphor?" he said as if speaking to himself. "An infinite sequence in mathematics can be defined using a recursive definition where one member of the sequence is defined by an operation on the last. That might serve as a surrogate for the effect of cause and effect."

"And you could run that process both forwards and backwards," mused Floyd. He took a piece of paper out of his pants pocket and wrote:

$$n_i = n_{i-1} + 1$$

He then wrote:

$$n_{i-1} = n_i - 1$$

So I can define any particular member in this sequence of numbers by referring either to a number ahead of it in the sequence or a number preceding it."

"That's true," said Al, "but if I ask you to 'give me a value for n_i' then you can't work out any of these expressions unless you have one member of the sequence which has a number. All you have is a formula for evaluating the next member of the sequence from the previous one. That formula is like our cause and effect world—each member of the sequence takes a previous term (read cause in the mathematical metaphor) and creates a new member of the sequence (read effect). This new effect becomes the cause for the next member of the sequence. You can't endlessly keep referring back to an early member of the sequence. The sequence will remain undefined until you find one member of the sequence that's a number and doesn't refer to another member. That single element anchors the whole sequence. That is Aristotle's uncaused cause. It's essential for the sequence to be defined."

"What if I put the concrete number in the middle and run the recursive definitions forward and backwards from it?" he mused. "I can see that won't help me since I have to explain where the number in the middle came from. Besides our world doesn't work that way. Future events can't cause events in the past since increasing entropy gives direction to the arrow of time."[20]

"I think you're right Floyd; trying to anchor the sequence in the middle doesn't solve the problem of the need for an uncaused cause, and as you pointed out, future events can't cause events in the past because time as a dimension has a direction to it."

"So what does that mean in terms of my sequence?" asked Floyd.

"I think it means you can't have an infinite sequence defined recursively where the founding term is infinitely displaced back in the sequence."

Floyd seemed unconvinced.

Al thought for a moment. "Let me try another approach. You're familiar with spreadsheets right?"

"Of course."

"Well," said Al, "in a spreadsheet one can define a cell content recursively by referring to another cell."

"Right!" said Floyd. "You mean defining say, cell A1000 by making it equal to the contents of cell A999 squared."

"You've got it," said Al. "But here's my point, you can't make the recursive definition go forward or backward an infinite number of times. There always has to be *one cell* that's not defined recursively and has to have a value or the whole recursive definition chain is undefined."

"I see what you mean," said Floyd. "There always has to be one cell with a value that the spreadsheet can calculate, on which the whole recursive sequence is built. This is good Al. It also explains away another

---

[20] Roger Penrose, *The Emperor's New Mind: Concerning Computers, Minds and the Laws of Physics* (Oxford, Oxford University Press, 1989).

idea I had. What if cause and effect were one giant cycle? What if one had a sequence of cause and effect that somehow bends back on itself so that an effect in the future causes an event in the distant past? I've heard some eastern philosophies have a cyclical view of time. If I apply your spreadsheet analogy, that would correspond to setting up a large circular reference, which again gives an error because the spreadsheet doesn't have a fixed cell to boot strap the whole cycle."

"You mean," said Al, "if you were to make cell A1000 equal to cell A999 all the way back to cell A1, you can't try to get around a fixed cell by making cell A1 equal to cell A1000."

"Right," said Floyd. "The whole series is undefined because the spreadsheet doesn't have a number to resolve all of the cell equalities."

"That," said Al, "is the Kalam argument as I understand it."

"Okay, I'll have to think about that. So where does that leave us?"

"As Aristotle pointed out, we need a first cause or a first mover in a cause and effect universe."

"There are many intelligent people who don't find the arguments for God compelling."

"That's true and 'presenting a cogent argument' is not the same as 'proving the argument.' Everyone has to decide which evidence is most compelling to them, and how much evidence is required before they consider something as proven. Often, the evidence we weight most strongly is influenced by our worldview.

"No matter how strong the argument, you can always claim 'I don't see the answer now, but I'm convinced as I examine the argument more closely, the flaw will appear,'" said Al.

"So you're saying you're not proving the existence of God, but presenting arguments for his existence?" asked Floyd.

"Right. Arguments are things we can talk about, but ultimately proof is something that happens in your mind," said Al. "In the end, accepting something as proved is a decision of the will. Another person can present all the evidence they want, but you can convince yourself that the evidence isn't enough, that they're not telling you everything, that the argument has a fatal flaw you just haven't seen yet, and so you're unconvinced. Proof happens in the mind."

SEVEN

Doesn't Neurochemistry Explain Our Belief in God?

O n Sunday afternoon, Al asked Floyd if he wanted to go sailing. "There's a good wind from the north and I've reserved a dinghy at the marina."

"I should be studying, but I can do that tonight. Where are we heading?"

"Since the wind is coming from the north. We should have an easy time leaving West Bay, and then we can tack north under the bridge and look for a sandbar or a small island for lunch."

"Sounds good to me."

"I have the provisions," said Al.

They walked to West Bay. Crossing the rise, the bay stretched out before them. West Bay was shaped like a cross-section diagram of the eye regularly featured in biology textbooks. The bay was about three quarters of a mile across. A gap to the West, where the pupil would have been, was straddled by Lighthouse Point and Causeway Point. Al found their dinghy about halfway down the quay. They loaded their supplies.

"All right if I take the tiller?" asked Floyd.

"Sure!"

Floyd settled in the stern while Al cast off the lines. The mainsail caught the breeze and Al sheeted the jib home. They completed a couple of short tacks and then settled on a course that would take them out of the bay. They hung out over the starboard side as the boat heeled over and cut a splendid bow wave.

"I'm back at our discussion again," Floyd shouted, trying to make himself heard over the wind.

"So what are you thinking?"

"Well I've been reading about neurochemistry and some of the advances that have been made in understanding human brain function. I think scientists have a pretty good idea why so many people believe in religion. Some have even described what's been termed the 'God gene[21].' I've heard about evidence that shows scientists can induce spiritual experiences by electrically stimulating certain parts of the brain[22]. I think they're showing that belief in religion is an adaptation that helps us survive."

"So how does that work?" asked Al.

"Well," continued Floyd, "there has, in the past, been a survival benefit to believing in religion. Thinking there is a father figure who is powerful, who will take care of us, helps relieve our primeval anxieties about our world. Those who don't have that stress are able to focus on other things, and so are more fit to survive than those who do."

"Where do these beliefs come from then?" asked Al.

"They're expressions of our genes manifested through our thoughts."

"And our thoughts, are they the product of chemistry?" asked Al.

"Why yes."

"So if some chemical reaction in our brain produces say chemical product A," asked Al, "we'll believe in God? And if it produces chemical product B instead, then we won't? Does that capture it?"

"I suppose so. Are you leading me on? Are you setting a trap?" asked Floyd.

"No. I'm trying to understand your position because I think it leads to a problem," responded Al.

"What problem?"

---

[21] Mario Beauregard & Denise O'Leary. *The Spiritual Brain* (New York, Harper Collins, 2007) pp. 50-55.
[22] Ibid. pp. 79-100.

"First of all," said Al, "you're ascribing our thoughts to chemistry. If all of our thoughts are the product of chemical reactions, you're basing all thought on irrational causes."

"What do you mean by irrational causes?" asked Floyd.

"Chemistry is chemistry," said Al. "There's no mind behind it. Precursors, enzymes, and rate constants determine the outcome. Why should that chemical outcome in any way be linked to reality? Why should I have any confidence that what my mind perceives is true or real? You're telling me it's really only linked to the chemistry, and chemistry is determined by principles of chemistry."

"Well if your mind were totally disconnected from reality, you couldn't survive," said Floyd.

"Bacteria and worms presumably have no mind, yet survive quite well. But even if I concede that in some cases there is a survival advantage to being linked to reality, you've presented me with a compelling counter example."

"How so?" asked Floyd.

"Well," said Al, "you just pointed out that almost all people through the ages have believed in God or gods, and secondly you've pointed out that this belief is an illusion, one that has in the past conferred a survival advantage on the believers of the illusion. Therefore it's become pervasive. In other words if you're optimizing *for survival*, you're not optimizing *for connection to reality*. Connection to reality will only occur when reality happens to confer a survival advantage to the organism and you've provided a pervasive example where this isn't the case. According to your statement, believing in a god, that is to say in an illusion, a non-reality, conveys a survival advantage on the believer. Perhaps there are many illusions like that, which confer survival advantages on those people who are deluded."

"I suppose," said Floyd slowly. "Why do I feel you're setting a trap for me after all?"

"What's especially troubling about this question," continued Al, "is that this explanation for why so many people have believed in God or gods is a question of the first importance. What could be more important than discovering if a Creator exists? If our thinking on that question is in jeopardy, isn't our thinking on all the lesser questions also highly suspect, except perhaps the simplest such as, 'Is that a predator?'"

They had passed the Lens and were sailing on a more even keel.

"Floyd, have you ever seen neurochemists turn their biochemical explanation to neurochemistry itself?"

"What do you mean Al?"

Perhaps the neurochemical explanation of thought can be analyzed using the same paradigm that neurochemists have applied to religion. Perhaps brain chemistry has produced chemicals in the brains of neurochemists, which led them to believe in the neurochemical basis of all thought because it gives them comfort and so confers a survival advantage on them."

"But Al, believing in God isn't the same as recognizing a predator. Failure to recognize a predator would lead to a quick death. Don't you see how survival guides our thoughts?"

"I see your point Floyd, but what about science and scientific observations? How are they linked to survival?"

"Science and technology have made us the true 'kings' of the plant and animal kingdom," said Floyd.

"I can see that, but I would've said inferential thought—the ability to state and test truth statements—is the real power behind science and observation. There are certainly technologies such as weapons, pesticides, and medicine, which have increased our species' ability to survive and even dominate our world. But do those survival advantages that apply to our species, really apply specifically to the scientists who developed them? Are scientists likely to produce more offspring than others because of the advances they've engineered? I don't see it. After all Floyd, you keep telling me how hard it will be for me, a science nerd, to find a date much less a wife."

"Okay, but you do concede that science through technology has conferred a significant survival advantage on us as a species?" asked Floyd.

"Some elements do, but not the parts that we find most profound or interesting," said Al. "Why would understanding the fundamentals of chemistry and physics convey a survival advantage? Wouldn't bows and arrows have been enough to dominate the plant and animal kingdom? What survival advantage does learning quantum chemistry confer on the learner? Will that ensure you have more offspring?"

"No it probably makes you unmarriageable," said Floyd. "It's the rare woman who wants to hear her husband prating on about energy levels, transition integrals and the Pauli Exclusion Principle. But we know they're true. We check them out, and experiments verify the results."

"But Floyd, in this discussion *our very thought* is on trial. If you conduct a neurochemical experiment on how people think, *you have to assume the reliability of your own thoughts* to design the experiment, to carry it out dispassionately, and finally to analyze the results. You're begging the questions because your thoughts—as well as everyone else's—are on trial. As C. S. Lewis once put it, it's like taking your eyeball out to look at it. It can't be done because the uncertainty, the contamination if you like, occurs at the source—our thoughts."

"So you're saying the neurochemists are wrong?" asked Floyd.

"In a way yes," said Al. "When neuroscientists are happily explaining away religion which they, as Materialists, see as a problem, they're explaining away every other thought as well, including their thinking behind neuroscience. They've sawn off the branch they're sitting on."

"I don't see it," said Floyd.

"Maybe a thought experiment would help," said Al. "In studying religion, neuroscientists measure brain response when people are praying or feeling religious feelings. Then they say, 'Ah ha! This chemical response in the brain gives rise to religious feelings, and therefore also to religion itself. I've now explained religion away and understand why so many people suffer under this illusion.[23]"

"You're coloring the debate with your language," said Floyd.

"Okay I'll gear back," said Al. "But consider applying the same technique to neuroscience itself. For example let's say two neurochemists study one another. When neurochemist A watches neurochemist B make a discovery and validate a hypothesis, he can see certain brain patterns emerge. If the hypothesis were realized to be invalid, different brain

---

[23] Mario Beauregard & Denise O'Leary, *The Spiritual Brain* (New York, HarperCollins, 2007).

chemistry would be observed. Now if neurochemist A were consistent, he'd say the same thing he said about religion: 'I know why B decided the way he did since I understand his brain chemistry.' When one chemical product is produced, he's convinced the hypothesis is true. If another is produced, the hypothesis is false. If the biochemical processes of the brain completely determine his thought, in this case the conclusion about the scientific hypothesis under scrutiny, then everything depends on the capriciousness of the chemistry."

"But science is true and religion is flaky!" exclaimed Floyd.

"I think you've found the core of the problem," said Al. "Neuroscientists never really apply their techniques to their own science. They implicitly *assume their thoughts and observations are uncontaminated by chemical determinism.* Their own thoughts reflect reality and so they're free to analyze and debunk the thoughts of others. They've artificially put themselves into a special category. That's neither right nor consistent."

"So what's your answer?" asked Floyd.

"As a Theist, I don't have that problem," said Al. "My own mind was created by God to be a reflection or image of his mind. So by design, I'm connected to reality. This is my own thought. I don't know if other Christians would agree with this, but I think every thought must, to some extent, be supernatural."

"I don't get why thought has to be supernatural," said Floyd.

"Well for genuine free will to exist, I mustn't be bound by cause and effect. If my physiological state *completely* determined my decisions, which has to happen in a closed cause and effect world, then all choice would be an illusion. I think there's a real me in my soul which injects my will into this body and mind from outside so that my thoughts are not determined by chemistry alone. Chemistry is the consequence not the determinant. Rather like throwing a rock into a pond; the rock comes from outside and causes the ripples. The observer only sees the ripples."

"You see," said Floyd, "that's what I don't like. Your position requires the supernatural, Al. But time and again, on closer examination, supernatural explanations give way to natural explanations."

"But don't you see Floyd that we're talking about the final step? If you explain away thought, you've explained away everything. Every step until now has preserved our humanity. When you take away thought, we're no more than machines programmed by our chemistry.[24]"

"Still," said Floyd, "we're so obviously affected by chemical inputs. We have drugs that can make you a gambler or calm you down. We have hallucinogens that can make you see things that aren't there. There are mental illnesses that cause people to kill their children or commit crimes. How do you reconcile that with free will?"

"Those are really good points," said Al. "In my own case I can see how moods, things I've read and events that have happened to me have affected my attitudes and decisions. Afterwards I wonder 'How could I have done and said that?'"

"Exactly my point," said Floyd.

"Let me think about it for a moment," said Al, as Floyd put the sailboat on the starboard tack. Al put his hand on his forehead, trying to get his thoughts in order. He knew what he wanted to say, but had trouble getting his ideas into a sequence that made sense.

"I guess Floyd, it all comes down to the meaning of free will or determinism. As I understand it, determinism, or the absence of free will, means there isn't a *single action*, or a *single thought* that isn't caused by physical or chemical stimulus. But the converse isn't true. To believe in free will, doesn't mean we're unaffected or impervious to genetics, disease, or even what we had for breakfast. These are influencers. But they don't determine the whole outcome. Indeed if they did determine the outcome, we couldn't be held responsible for our actions. That's why we have a legal test for accountability for our actions; why accused people sometimes have to be declared 'fit' to stand trial. So even though we're a psychosomatic whole, such that our bodies and our chemistry do affect us a lot, they're not the complete story. Inside us there's a part that really lets us make genuine decisions in spite of the tendencies or predilections our bodies and our chemistries impose on us. In fact part of the role of education is to help us become *less influenced* by these extraneous stimuli so that our judgment responds to the data and not to what we had for breakfast."

---

[24] C. S. Lewis, *The Abolition of Man* (London, HarperCollins, 1999), p. 42.

"Well, maybe that's all an illusion," said Floyd. "I read a book that argued against free will and it seemed to me the author could show how that's all an illusion; we think we're deciding, but we're not. It's all been determined by our genes, our biochemistry, and our environment.[25]"

Al was warming to the discussion. "Let me illustrate what I mean. Let's say, for example that you go to a party and have far too much to drink. You make a fool of yourself. The next morning you go to your friends and apologize saying 'I wasn't myself last night because I had too much to drink.' When you say that, you're saying it wasn't really you that others were seeing. They were seeing actions determined by the alcohol."

"What about this book I read on free will and the idea that free will is an illusion."

"If there is no such thing as free will, why did the author bother writing a book about the subject?"

"What do you mean? He was making an argument, as you are," said Floyd.

"But 'making an argument,' means he was evaluating data and writing conclusions based on what the data showed. But that requires free will. If the whole argument in the book were determined *completely by his genetic makeup* and another author with a different genetic makeup would be *compelled* to write a book arguing *for* free will why should we believe either of them? They have nothing of importance to say. Arguments and all science would be reduced to another example of gene expression, like hair color."

Floyd leaned back on the tiller and said nothing for a while. Then he perked up and pointed.

"Look at that low island over there, Al. Are you getting hungry?"

Nodding, Al climbed out on the bow to get a better look. "I think there's a small cove off our port bow. A short tack should bring us in."

---

[25] Sam Harris, *Free Will* (New York: Free Press, 2012).

EIGHT

Hasn't Evolution Disproved Christianity?

Floyd expertly maneuvered their dinghy into the cove. Al released the jib, then plunged into the surf to haul the boat up onto the beach as Floyd lowered the mainsail. Al tied the painter to some driftwood above the high tide mark, and then went back for his cooler and backpack from the dry bow compartment in the dinghy. They trekked up the sandy beach to a dell sheltered from the north wind by a spine of rock. The wind had picked up, and whitecaps flecked the green sea. Al took a deep breath, reveling in the tang of seaweed in the air. He unpacked cold pizza for their meal. Meanwhile, Floyd built a small fire in a pit left by previous visitors. When the fire was burning merrily, Al passed the pizza to Floyd, then sat back, munching on his own piece thoughtfully.

Pizza is almost as good cold as it is hot. I'm so hungry.

They ate in silence. Al looked toward the Atlantic.

Nothing but water from here to Europe.

He looked up and saw that Floyd was finishing his piece. "Floyd, there's one piece left. Would you like it?"

"No Al, I'm stuffed. Too bad we don't have any coffee."

"Ah but we do." Al brought out an old metal percolator, filled it with water from his water jug and balanced it on two logs in the fire. He filled the insert with ground coffee, then moved to take the lid off.

"Ow! That's already hot."

"Are you okay?"

"Yes I'm fine. I just feel stupid. I don't think it will even raise a blister."

He used a towel to position the pot on the fire, and then sat back sucking his burned fingers. Floyd gazed over the surf, looking out toward the east. Al followed Floyd's gaze.

How beautiful the ocean looks! It's as if it were made for me to enjoy. It's a work of art.

Floyd interrupted his thoughts. "As I was looking out over the ocean, I thought about how the world and everything in it came about. It reminded me I wanted to ask you about Genesis and evolution."

"Ask away," Al invited.

"Earlier, when we were talking about neurochemistry and our thought processes, you raised an interesting point. You talked about the evolution of thought. I had the distinct sense that you don't believe in the Theory of Evolution."

"Floyd, I want to be a truth-seeker. That means I have to be willing to follow the evidence wherever it leads."

"Okay, Al, but you didn't really answer my question. Do you believe in the Theory of Evolution?"

"Floyd, I've been part of these discussions often enough to know that there's great potential for misunderstanding because the topic of evolution itself seems to raise passions."

"But Al, I asked a simple question. Do you believe the Theory of Evolution? Can't you give me a 'yes' or a 'no' answer?"

"It's not that simple."

"Why not? I get the feeling you're evading my question."

"Probably. First of all, discussions about evolution are, for the most part, discussions about secondary questions, not primary questions like the question about God's existence. Secondly, there's been so much bad press and misinformation about the whole subject I think it's difficult to have a rational discussion. So I prefer to avoid talking about it since it doesn't bring people one millimeter closer to meeting the reality of God."

"Hmm. Maybe you're avoiding the discussion because you don't have any good answers," said Floyd.

Al sighed. "I don't think so Floyd, but I'm happy to have you correct me if that's the case."

"Well I don't want to let you off the hook," said Floyd. "If you read the first chapter of Genesis, you read all of this hocus pocus about the Spirit of God hovering over the waters, of light before stars and the sun, of creation in six days.[26] We've disproven all of that. We know life on this planet began about two to three billion years ago as single-celled organisms, and then over time all other life forms evolved from that early state. How can you believe anything you read in the Bible when it's so clearly wrong on this point?"

"So we know all that, do we?" said Al. "I personally don't think as far as theories go, that the Theory of Evolution is on very sound footing," said Al.

"How can you say that Al? It's the foundation of biology and biochemistry!"

"Is it? Why do you say that?" asked Al.

"It explains the similarities between organisms," continued Floyd, "it explains unusual species proliferation such as in the Galapagos and Australia. It's foundational to everything."

"I don't see that," said Al. "When I read Michael Behe's book *Darwin's Black Box*[27], I was astounded to read the Theory of Evolution is always presented on par or exceeding the importance and explanatory power of Quantum Theory, Atomic Theory, or the success of Maxwell's equations. But then, Behe went on to say that although evolution is always present as absolutely critical to the existence of biology and chemistry as disciplines, when you look closely, it's really only used for introductions to papers and conclusions where authors speculate on the evolutionary history of an organism or an enzyme system. The theory has no predictive power."

"That can't be right," said Floyd.

"Okay," said Al, "let's try to make an evolutionary prediction. What will be the next step in human evolution and when will it occur?"

---

[26] Genesis 1:1-31.

[27] Michael J. Behe, *Darwin's Black Box. The Biochemical Challenge to Evolution* (New York, The Free Press, 1996), p. 179.

"Years ago I read somewhere," said Floyd thoughtfully, "that women are getting shorter and squatter because it makes them better at child bearing.[28]"

"Are women flattered by that prediction?" Al smiled.

Floyd picked up another stick, snapped it and thrust it into the fire. "I doubt it. I wouldn't presume to speak for their sex, but the long-term prospect of being shorter and squatter as an aid to childbearing wouldn't have appealed to any of the women I know. Still it's a documented prediction."

"The inconsistency of those trends with current views aside, let's assume the data presented is accurate," said Al. "Those speculations about our species' evolution are based on extrapolations from current, very short-term trends. But my point is the theory doesn't tell us the answer, and we don't expect the theory to tell us the answer. At least not in the way that atomic theory predicts chemical structure, or quantum theory predicts ionization potentials. Certainly if women did get progressively shorter and squatter, the theory would rationalize the change in terms of biological advantage. But rationalization is a far cry from prediction. If women became taller and thinner instead, then a new explanation also invoking biological advantage for the data would be readily at hand. The Theory of Evolution is wonderful at providing hand-waving explanations for any data that comes along, but simply doesn't have the explanatory power of quantum mechanics or of Maxwell's Equations."

"Al, it seems to me you're evading the issue. Is a six-day creation more in line with our data than an evolutionary explanation? How can you trust the Bible if it's so wrong about this issue?"

"The simple answer is that I'm not sure the Bible is wrong. As far back as the fourth century, Augustine, the bishop of Hippo, wanted to write two explanatory works on the early chapters of Genesis, one which took the passage literally and one where he took that passage figuratively. As I recall, he wrote the figurative one first because it was easiest. How to understand Genesis is not a new problem. It's been under discussion since long before the Theory of Evolution came along."

---

[28] Katie Engelhart, *Evolution favours shorter and heavier women—like it or not. Natural selection is still at work* (MacLeans, Thursday March 18, 2010).

"So what about it, do you believe in The Theory of Evolution?"

"I suppose that depends on what you mean."

"How so?" asked Floyd.

"The first step in any discussion is to get the definitions clear, unambiguous and co-extensive with the property being discussed. So Floyd, when you use the word evolution, what exactly do you mean?"

"Evolution," said Floyd, "means changes in an organism that occur over time."

"Is that all it means?" asked Al.

"What are you getting at, Al?"

"Well, there's often an implicit part of the definition that's left unsaid. For example small changes caused by random mutations that accumulate are said to lead to the huge diversity that we find in the plant and animal kingdom. Some go on to point out these changes occur solely by chance without the intervention of design of any kind."

"I suppose that's my position."

"My point," said Al, "is that those are *three very different definitions*. For example the simplest definition 'change over time' is so trivial that pretty well everyone, on reflection, would agree with it, so if that's your definition we're all evolutionists."

"Go on," said Floyd.

"At the other end of the spectrum, the definition that explicitly insists on chance, and rules out design or the intervention of God, is a *metaphysical statement, and is not empirically verifiable*. One cannot design an experiment that definitively rules out the intervention of an intelligence. Therefore so much depends on the definition.[29]

"Floyd, I think everyone is an evolutionist for definition one; some Christians are evolutionists according to definition two[30], but I can't see how a Christian could be an evolutionist according to definition three, affirming that our world arose completely by chance without any direction or intervention by God."

---

[29] Peter Kreeft and Ronald K. Tacelli, *Handbook of Christian Apologetics* (Downers Grove, IVP Academic, 1994), p. 218.

[30] Francis S. Collins, *The Language of God* (New York, Simon & Schuster, 2007).

"So where do you stand, Al?"

"As I said Floyd, I'm willing to believe whatever the evidence shows. There was a time when I was an evolutionist and thought it was compatible with belief in God. I now believe the Theory of Evolution is in serious trouble.

"I guess I've come to believe in what I call The Law of Conservation of Complexity," Al explained. "Living organisms, even if you treat them as chemical machines, are incredibly complex. As we've studied them, each step in the discovery process has led to greater layers of complexity. Materialists, wedded to explaining all of this by chance without any intervention and direction by God, keep refining descriptions that show these come about by a process driven by chance. But it seems to me they're simply moving the complexity from the process to the system. The complexity doesn't go away—it can't."

Floyd sighed and ran his hand over his shaven head. "Al, you're outta your tree. There's almost universal agreement among everyone who counts that the theory is rock solid. You're committing scientific and intellectual suicide by believing that Intelligent Design garbage."

"Floyd, you're telling me it's unpopular, even detrimental from a career perspective to deny the validity of the Theory of Evolution, but all of your evidence so far has amounted to appeals to authority. So why do you believe it? How much of the Theory have you personally investigated?"

"The evidence is all around me. I see bacteria developing immunity to antibiotics. Insects become more tolerant to pesticides. When I go to the Museum of Natural History, I see dinosaur skeletons and fossils. All of this is evidence for evolution in progress."

"The only evidence that we can actually see happening, such as bacteria developing immunity to antibiotics, is support for only the simplest, most unassuming definition for evolution, that is 'change of any kind.' But that's not evidence for the changes required to explain the diversity we see in life," said Al.

"But those changes are merely accumulations of those microscopic changes," insisted Floyd.

"That doesn't work for me Floyd. Let's say we want to evolve by random chance from species A to species B by incremental changes.

Then one can put any number of intermediate steps together as steps in a sequence to get to B. Al used a stick to draw a sequence in the sand: $A=>A_1=>A_2 \ldots A_n=>B$. If we choose enough intermediate steps such that the changes in the sequence are very small, then the random chance of coming up with, say, A_1 has a reasonable probability. However A_n has to have a survival advantage over A_{n-1} and so on back over the sequence. Otherwise the principle of Survival of the Fittest will kill A_n off. I don't think we can even identify these intermediate steps."

"Okay, Al, you and the other Intelligent Design folks are playing the same game that you've always played. You've identified a gap in our knowledge, so you want to rule out the whole theory because there are some gaps. But history has shown we've filled in the gaps time and again, and then you folks simply form a new defensive line based on some new gaps."

"Yes, I know about the 'God of the gaps' counter argument," said Al wearily. "However, it looks to me that what I'm questioning is not an inconsequential gap, but the central thesis of the whole evolutionary argument, namely that one can achieve macroscopic changes by accumulating small ones. What I'm hearing is that we can't observe the large changes because too much time is required. And yet, one cannot even conceptually map out—on a chemical basis—what links in the chemical chain would bring about the macroscopic change from one species to another. Maybe we should wait until we have at least worked *that* out before flaunting this theory. We should wait until we have the evidence."

"You always want more evidence," said Floyd, his voice rising. "We have a mountain of evidence already. What about the fossil record? Look how many extinct species we've dug up. Everything can be put into a pattern."

"I think," said Al, "that if scientists were as skeptical about their own theory as they are about Intelligent Design, they would acknowledge that the fossil record raises as many problems for the Theory of Evolution as it solves."

"Where do you get that from?" asked Floyd.

"Go back to my sequence A transforming into B. We need the intermediate forms A_1 to A_n to make the problem tractable from a probability stand point, but time and again we see A and B in the fossil record but not A_1 to A_n. Why not? We've already shown that A_n has to be better adapted to its environment than A_{n-1} and also better than A. Why don't we see them? Why do we see only A and B?"

"Your argument is as old as the hills," said Floyd vehemently. "It's the 'no transitional forms' argument. That's exactly what I mean by 'God in the gaps.' We *have found* intermediate forms. The most recent I'm aware of is the one they found in northern Canada."

"You mean the fossil found in the Canadian arctic *Tiktaalik roseae*, that is thought to represent a transitional form from fish to tetrapods?[31]"

"Yeah, that's the one."

"But look what we see and what's missing," said Al. "Every branch in the tree of life ought to have dozens, perhaps hundreds of intermediate forms, each of which has some survival advantage over the node in the branch. Instead of a tree of life, we ought to have a cloud of life with each species having many nearest neighbors. It just doesn't add up to me."

"The fact is," said Floyd, "life is here in all its complexity. If not evolution, then tell me how we got here. And don't say 'God.' I want a mechanistic explanation based on biochemistry."

"Floyd, we all agree life is here in all its complexity. The question is how life arose. Saying 'I want a mechanistic explanation based on biochemistry' is possible as long as you don't add the constraint that it can only happen by random undirected processes."

"Why not? Isn't that what science studies?" insisted Floyd.

"If you insist the process has to be random, you're begging the question," said Al. "How do we even know what 'random' looks like, unless we have some idea what a designed system is like? I can tell a sand dune is random because I've seen a sand castle that was designed and molded by an artist. The same question arises here."

"So where does that leave us?" asked Floyd.

"I read a book by William Dembski called *The Design Inference*," said Al. "In it, he outlined a test for distinguishing a designed structure from

---

[31] "Tiktaalik" http://en.wikipedia.org/wiki/Tiktaalik/

a random structure. He talked about improbability and the specification required to demonstrate that a structure is designed.[32]"

"How does that work?" asked Floyd.

"Well," said Al, "take a five card poker hand. Every hand you deal will be equally improbable. Let's see if I can remember by combinatorial statistics. If I deal a five card hand from a deck of 52 cards, then there are 52 ways of choosing the first card, 51 for the second down to 48 for the fifth."

"Right," said Floyd. "Let me dig out my calculator. That's fifty-two factorial divided by forty-seven factorial. I get 311,875,200 combinations."

"Sounds right," said Al. "Dembski makes the point that each hand you deal is equally improbable, so having an improbable hand is not especially interesting. But let's say you were playing an opponent in poker and he was dealt three spade royal flushes in a row. Wouldn't you suspect he was a card-sharp and controlled the deal? So what's happened? The rules of poker add *a specification*, that ranks various hands in terms of their value for winning the pot, and select only four of the combinations as being the very best. So it's the combination of having very many possible hands, all equally improbable by random chance, together with a specification determined before the hand was dealt—a royal flush— that works to make the result very improbable."

"I follow you so far, Al. If the universe is 13 billion years old, we have a whole lot of hands to deal to get the right probability to come up."

"Not according to Dembski," said Al. "Probabilities are highly nonlinear. He came up with a very, very conservative probability test based on the number of particles in the universe and the time allowed, and came up with a design criterion of roughly one part in 10 to the power of 150. If a random event is more improbable than that fraction, then one can conclude that one can't reasonably expect that event to arise by chance."

"Al you're my friend and I know you're sincere, but if you continue talking like this I'm worried it will impact your career. If our profs hear

[32] William A. Dembski, *The Design Inference. Eliminating Chance Through Small Probabilities* (Cambridge, Cambridge University Press, 1998).

you talking like this, you'll lose all credibility. It'll affect your grades and your ability to get a job. I'm your friend and I care about what happens to you. Keep your thoughts to yourself."

"I know Floyd, I know," said Al wistfully. "Our educational system is so uniformly against any hint of design that students come out of it believing that anyone who questions the Theory of Evolution is anti-science and an idiot. I wish the system wouldn't put such barriers in front of me. I want to decide for myself based on the evidence. I shouldn't have to worry that my honest enquiry might cost me my job, or prevent me from being accepted for a teaching position. But there it is. I have to be true to myself. I must follow the evidence wherever it leads."

"I'm still worried it's going to keep you from getting a job," said Floyd.

"Yes, I know," said Al. "It's unfair. I can function perfectly well as a chemist or biochemist by simply knowing the chemistry. Evolution plays no functional role in those disciplines and I only get into trouble if I engage in conversations like this one. Still don't you see how we've stopped talking about evidence and started talking about the consequences of not following the consensus of the establishment? If the Theory of Evolution is so compelling, why this need to silence the critics? Why not just keep presenting the evidence? I think all of this talk meant to stifle debate—especially in the classroom—is a thinly-veiled admission that the ground on which the theory rests is pretty shaky, and that if students hear the critical questions being asked and the paucity of answers given, they'll lose respect for the theory."

Floyd looked up. "I don't like the look of those clouds. We'd better pack up."

NINE

The Storm

Al washed the utensils and food containers in the surf and loaded his knapsack. Floyd brought the rest of their supplies from the camp and began getting the dinghy ready for launch. Al looked up apprehensively. Black clouds had rolled in and the air had the electric smell of a storm. The wind had picked up and was blowing in gusts from different directions.

"Can we make it back before the storm hits, do you think?" asked Al.

"I don't know, but I don't think we can stay here. This island is too low. We've got to try to make it back."

After stowing their gear, Floyd climbed into the stern and took the tiller while Al pushed them into the surf. Al brought the bow into deeper water. Floyd raised the mainsail as Al clambered onto the bow. They picked up way as Floyd put the wind on the starboard quarter. Al was able to raise the jib and they plowed through two-foot waves. With full sail, they shot through the water. Clouds rolled in and the rain poured down. Visibility was now less than a hundred feet as the gusting wind whipped spray into their faces. Floyd had the grim concentration of a man who knew his life was in danger, and any lack of focus could end it all.

"Al!" shouted Floyd, "Help me lower the sail!"

Al gave him the "thumbs up" and lowered the jib while crawling forward on the bow to bring the sail in and lash it to the stay. Then he crawled back amidships, shifting his weight to compensate for the gusting wind.

Al pointed to the mainsail. Floyd nodded and Al began to lower the mainsail and then slab-reef it to reduce the wind resistance. After one reef, Floyd gave the thumbs up.

Floyd's good. He changes our course in the wave trough to help us climb the waves, and then adjusts when we catch more wind on the crest.

The wind veered again and the boom swung to the port side. The dinghy listed badly and Al flung himself to the windward side. The dinghy teetered on the edge of going over—with Al hanging out as far as he could—when Floyd adjusted their course to ease the pressure on the sail.

Lightning flashes lit up the clouds in the west. The rain came down in sheets. Visibility was now only about fifty feet. They plowed on.

I hope this weather breaks. I've lost all sense of direction. Lord, get us out of this.

Another tremendous gust of wind came from an unexpected quarter, and the boom again swung to the other side. Al tried to duck, but he was too slow. He felt a flash of pain as the boom hit his shoulder, sending him careening forward into the water.

He closed his mouth. Everything went dark. Al felt the mast and rigging at his back. Ropes floated around him like stinger tentacles on a Portuguese Man-of-War.

The dinghy must have gone over after I fell in.

He tried to swim out, but a rope was tangled around his ankle. He tried to reach down to free his ankle, but something had snagged the back of his life jacket. In desperation, he bent his knee with all his might. The rope cut into his skin and tightened. He couldn't get his hand down to reach the rope. Whatever had snagged the back of his life jacket held firm.

Fear seized him like a cold fist. He tried again and again to no avail. His lungs screamed for air.

I'm almost done. I can't hold my breath any longer. Lord I'm coming home.

He felt a tug on his back, as Floyd desperately pulled him back and forth, trying to unsnag him. Floyd began to undo Al's life jacket.

What an idiot I am. Why didn't I think of that!

Al helped and was soon free. The two worked to release Al's ankle and then surfaced beside the dinghy, gasping for air.

"Whatever you do Al, don't let go of the dinghy," Floyd panted between gulps of air.

Al nodded. He couldn't speak. The dinghy turtled, floating mast down, centerboard up.

The two men grabbed the centerboard and together hoisted themselves out of the water. Their combined weight tipped the dinghy back onto its side.

"Stay on the centerboard, Al. We need to get her upright."

Al kept his body weight across the centerboard while Floyd worked his way to the other side of the dinghy. In a few seconds a rope flew across the dinghy and Al caught it and pulled it tight. Floyd reappeared.

"Let's see if we can get the mast out of the water," said Floyd.

Together they hauled on the rope, bracing against the centerboard. Slowly the mast cleared the water. When she started to move, Floyd let go and swam around to the other side. Seeing she would tumble home, Al also released and grabbed the gunwale. With Al on one side, and Floyd on the other, the dinghy rolled ponderously in the water.

"I've got her," shouted Floyd over the wind. "Why don't you try to climb in the stern and start bailing? In this swell, with this much water in her, she's ready to go over again."

Al hoisted himself onto the stern. He watched Floyd shift more to the bow to balance his own weight. The rain had eased up a bit. Bailing vigorously, Al soon had water flying out of the dinghy.

"I think we have enough free board now. Why don't you climb in? I'll stay low to steady her," said Al.

Floyd moved to the stern, waited until she crested a wave, then swung himself into the dinghy where he crouched on the bottom with Al. They bailed for another five minutes, before Floyd pulled a paddle from the sealed storage compartment and tied it to a painter, then flung it behind them as a sea anchor.

"Now we wait, hope and pray we don't encounter any shoals," said Floyd.

"Hope and pray?" asked Al.

"It's only an expression. You know what I mean," said Floyd.

"By the way, Floyd—thanks. I thought I was a goner for sure."

"Don't mention it," said Floyd. "But see, Atheists aren't so bad. I came to look for you when you didn't pop up."

"Yes," said Al, "how very un-Darwinian of you. Logically you should have let me die, reveling in the fact that your progeny wouldn't encounter any competition from my progeny."

"Actually," said Floyd, "the thought of progeny never came up. Anyways I have to keep reminding you that a nerd like you would never be competition on the progeny front for a jock like me."

Al laughed. "I keep forgetting. Still I'm glad you acted better than your Darwinian principles and rescued me.

Al sensed the motion of the boat had lessened. He peeked out from under the sail. There was a sliver of light in the west. The rain had stopped. The clouds were passing.

Floyd also looked out. "Maybe fifteen minutes more and we could risk making sail," he observed.

Al breathed a sigh of relief. Quiet for a few minutes, they listened only to the wind and the waves.

"Our conversation on the island was interrupted by the storm," said Floyd. "Did we resolve anything?

"I don't know. We've had a chance to talk about a good many things this past week. Have you had any final impressions?" asked Al.

"You mean 'did you convert me?' No you didn't. So what about you? Did you finally see the light and become an Atheist?"

"No, I didn't become an Atheist" Al chuckled. "I did learn a few things through listening to your objections though. I was also able to get to know you much better by talking about important things, even if we didn't agree on the essential elements. And you?"

"I also learned a few things I'd never heard before," said Floyd. "I'm still astounded by our discussion today about the Theory of Evolution. I'm flabbergasted you don't believe it."

"I know. I hear that rather often," said Al.

"All of our talk about changing our minds reminds me of an argument for atheism that I had read and found rather compelling," said Floyd.

"Go on. I'm listening," said Al.

"The ancient Greeks believed in many gods. Then Christians, who are presumably more enlightened, came to believe in one God. Why not follow this logical progression of enlightenment, go the next step, and do away with God or gods altogether? Become a Materialist.[33]"

"I can see your progression," said Al, "but I don't see how that amounts to a proof."

"Still, it shows a trajectory of enlightenment, doesn't it?"

"You see," said Al, "I would have stated it differently. Christians were not the first to come up with the idea of one God. That idea is Jewish, and as far as I know, that may have been the original view. With one God, I have a perfect being, a single first mover. That gives rise to everything else. The Greeks and others had many gods, who were less than perfect, even though they were more powerful than mere mortals. Now Materialists come along and claim there are no gods. So who's left at the top of the heap? *Homo sapiens*. Man may not be termed a 'god' by Materialists, but he serves the same function. The real progression, it seems to me, is that as we move away from the all-powerful Creator of Judeo-Christian understanding, the gods become more numerous as they become weaker. We're really moving from One God, to dozens in Hellenistic thought, to seven billion in the case of Materialists."

I suppose that's another point of view," said Floyd.

"Your question, asking if I had become an Atheist as the result of our discussion, has set me to thinking. Although I listened to your arguments and I think I understood them, they never really led me to question my faith. I guess it's like hearing a friend argue that I don't have a mother, that my memories are all a sham, and that I was really brought up in an orphanage."

"Go on," said Floyd. He was keeping a sharp eye on the storm, especially the waves.

---

[33] Richard Dawkins, *The God Delusion* (New York: Houghton Mifflin, 2006).

"I've met my mother and she's a real person," said Al. "That concrete experience supersedes all arguments. Similarly I've had real experiences with the Lord Christ. Those personal experiences provide much more direct evidence to me than any argument. It probably doesn't carry much weight with you, but it's direct evidence for me."

Floyd turned to Al as if gaining special interest in Al's last statement.

"But Al, how do you reconcile that with your earlier statement that 'you questioned your way to faith?' It seems to me now you're saying your faith is based on this personal anecdotal evidence that means nothing to me.

Al took his glasses out of his pocket and cleaned them. "Floyd, for me, I had to use reason to answer a bunch of questions that stood in my way. That's what I meant by 'I questioned my way to faith.' Actually there aren't a lot of Christians who even care about the questions that bothered me a lot. I guess we're not all the same. For me I had to 'run the ramp of reason before I took the leap of faith.[34]' Faith always comes down to a decision to trust and so it has inherent uncertainty associated with it, as do all relationships. Reason can only take you so far. But getting that far makes it possible to trust."

Al shifted his position to correct for a slight list in the boat. "So where does this leave us, Floyd? Did our conversations help with your questions about your grandmother's faith?"

"Yeah, it did help Al. I had felt a palpable disappointment that my grandmother was irrational because of her expressed faith. You've convinced me that your position and hers are not irrational, just a different weighting of the evidence."

"Well, Floyd, I guess most important to me was that we were able to talk about an area of major disagreement and still part as friends."

"Yeah me too."

Al smiled and tightened up the jib. "Let's make sail. I think that haze on the horizon is Halcyon. We have a long way to go before we're home. But at least we're under way."

---

[34] Bruxy Cavey. *Sermon Podcast of The Meeting House.* http://www.themeeting-house.com/.

THE END

Discussion Questions

1. **Chapter 1 Questioning Your Way to Faith**
1. Can you think of any examples from your own life, or the lives of those close to you, where a crisis made you re-evaluate your beliefs or worldview? Why do you think this happens?
2. Is your definition of faith the same as Al's? To what extent do you agree with his definition?
3. Do you think science and faith are complementary or contradictory? Why do you hold that position?
4. Can you think of examples of how Jesus provided reasons for trust as he interacted with his disciples and the people around him? Do you accept the fact that he was evidential in his approach?
5. If you were to make a list of things that science alone doesn't explain, what would be on your list?
6. Have you ever learned from someone with whom you strongly disagreed? What made that possible?

2. **Chapter 2 The Importance of Questions**
1. Are any questions about the nature of God important to you?
2. How do you fit faith and questioning together?
3. Are you a person whom your friends could question? What could you do to be more open to questions?

4. What faith-related questions have troubled you the most? Have you found any answers?

5. Culture has moved from an era of modernism (having the best and most complete explanation wins) to postmodernism (everyone has a valid story; there is no absolute truth). How have these two perspectives influenced our attitudes to questions?

3. **CHAPTER 3 THE PROBLEM OF EVIL**

1. Floyd thinks there is an inherent contradiction in "the three omnies." Do you agree or disagree with him? Why?

2. How would you respond to Al's contention that if we had merely evolved in this world, we wouldn't be so strongly in reaction against it?

3. What did you think of Al's "Is anything wrong with anything" argument?

4. Floyd contends there is no God and Al then responds, "Then there is no evil either." Do you think Al is correct? Why or why not?

5. Do you find yourself getting angry as you debate about these central issues? Where does the anger come from? How do you combat it?

4. **CHAPTER 4 TWO KINDS OF QUESTIONS**

1. Did Jesus react negatively to questions? Can you think of some examples from the New Testament where God, an angel, or perhaps Jesus reacted negatively to questions? When were questions appreciated?

2. What did you think of the anecdote of the politician stopping to help a motorist as a publicity stunt? How would you have reacted?

3. What do you think about the three types of morality talked about by C. S. Lewis? Do you think this analysis is valid?

4. How has power replaced morality as we enforce laws? Are we moving more in that direction? What evidence do you see for and against that trend?

5. Do you believe morality is a universal standard or a personal invention? How does your point of view affect what you do and how you view others?

5. **CHAPTER 5 THE PROBLEM OF EVIL COMMITTED BY CHRISTIANS**
1. What do you think is the origin of religious conflict?
2. Al argues that there is a bias in applying a religious motivation to past deeds. Do you think he's right or wrong? Why?
3. Al also argues that tyrants have to appeal to a "good" to justify "evil." Do you think that is true?
4. If religion was once a value worth defending, what values have taken its place in our society?
5. How do you find the balance between defending important values, and not becoming a dupe for a tyrant?

6. **CHAPTER 6 THE PROBLEM OF PHYSICAL CALAMITY**
1. How do you explain calamity?
2. How do you respond to Al's contention that if we grew up out of this world we wouldn't be so much in reaction against it?
3. If you believe in heaven, do you think there will be danger and excitement there? Why or why not?
4. How do you react toward philosophical arguments for God? Are they interesting or do you not care?
5. Did the Kalam argument make sense or not?

7. **CHAPTER 7 DOESN'T NEUROCHEMISTRY EXPLAIN OUR FAITH IN GOD?**
1. Have you heard about the "God Helmet" in the media? What was your reaction?
2. Al makes the point that explaining away thought is different from explaining away everything else. Do you agree or disagree with him? Why?
3. Have you ever experienced a chemically induced change in behaviour? How did it feel from the inside?

8. CHAPTER 8 HASN'T EVOLUTION DISPROVED CHRISTIANITY?

1. What has been your journey on the debate about the Theory of Evolution?

2. What is your definition for evolution?

3. Al talked about the importance of clarifying definitions. Did that argument make sense to you? How might the art of clarifying definitions shed light on the discussion if you are ever drawn into a debate on this subject?

4. How have debates on the subject of evolution proceeded in the past for you?

5. Have you read much on Intelligent Design? What do you think about the discussion on that subject?

9. CHAPTER 9 THE STORM

1. When Floyd saved Al's life, was that inconsistent or consistent with Floyd's atheistic beliefs? Why or why not?

2. Al pointed out that Floyd's action was "un-Darwinian." Do you think that was true?

3. What can you do to resolve to have thoughtful and respectful discussions with people who disagree with you?

4. What does a respectful discussion look like?

5. What do you think motivates a moral atheist to be moral?

Suggestions for Further Reading

Beauregard, Mario and O'Leary, Denise. *The Spiritual Brain. A Neuroscientist's Case for the Existence of the Soul.* New York, HarperOne, 2007.

Behe, Michael J. *Darwin's Black Box. The Biochemical Challenge to Evolution.* New York, The Free Press, 1996.

Dembski, William A. *The Design Inference. Eliminating Chance Through Small Probabilities.* Cambridge, Cambridge University Press, 2007.

Gonzalez, Guillermo and Richards, Jay W. *The Privileged Planet. How Our Place in the Cosmos is Designed for Discovery.* Washington, D.C., Regnery Publishing Inc., 2004.

Kreeft, Peter and Tacelli, Ronald K. *Handbook of Christian Apologetics.* Downer's Grove, Illinois, Intervarsity Press, 1994.

Lewis, C. S. *Mere Christianity.* New York, Touchstone, 1996.

Lewis, C. S. *Miracles.* New York, HarperCollins, 1996.

Lewis, C. S. *The Abolition of Man.* London, Fount Paperbacks, 1978.

THE HALCYON DISLOCATION

Floyd and Al are characters taken from the futuristic thriller called *The Halcyon Dislocation*. If you would like to read more about Floyd and Al, here are a few sample chapters from that novel.

ONE

The Dislocation

Dave Schuster sat in the chancellor's office drinking coffee. The conversation had lapsed. Pushing back a strand of unruly black hair, Dave looked at his uncle across the desk and waited, respectfully, for the older man to say something.

Chancellor Charles O'Reilly lounged back in his chair. Fifty-three and clean-shaven with gray hair, O'Reilly had maintained his trim military build. While admiral of America's Sixth Fleet, he'd had few opportunities to visit Dave's home. Nevertheless he still enjoyed a close relationship with his sister, Dave's mother. With O'Reilly's recent retirement from the navy, his appointment to the University of Halcyon as chancellor, and Dave's arrival as an engineering student, they had determined to get to know each other better. However, the demands of the chancellorship and the frenetic pace of first year engineering had conspired to make this visit—on Wednesday, March 2—their first since Dave had arrived to live on the island campus in September.

"Are you still interested in astronomy?" O'Reilly asked warmly, gazing at his nineteen year old nephew.

Dave was jarred from his train of thought. "Yeah, I am. I didn't bring my telescope, but I still can't get enough of it."

"If you love it so much, why did you go into engineering?"

"I didn't think I could get a job in astronomy," Dave laughed. At six feet two inches tall, with the broad shouldered physique of a linebacker, Dave was as large as he was practical.

O'Reilly rubbed an old scar on his chin. Suddenly, he bolted upright in his chair. Dave followed his uncle's eyes and stared through the large balcony doors across from the desk. Angry gray storm clouds had replaced the bright sunlight of only a few minutes ago. Immediately, a flash of lightning followed by a crash of thunder rent the air. The lightning lit up the room in a dazzling display, as one bolt followed another in rapid, artillery-barrage succession.

"What in the world—" began O'Reilly.

A bright flash of red light blazed through the glass doors, giving way a moment later to a tremendous shock wave. The room shuddered. Several books fell to the floor from the shelf behind O'Reilly's oak desk. Dave's stomach lurched as if he were falling through the floor.

Startled, both men jumped to their feet and moved to the glass doors. Half a mile distant, a fireball rose from the experimental field in the center of the island campus. Smoke from the explosion had already begun to obscure their view.

The phone rang. O'Reilly darted back to his desk.

"O'Reilly!" he barked. He listened, grim-faced, to the caller, only occasionally grunting assent into the mouthpiece.

Placing the receiver on the cradle, his eyes hard, he squared his shoulders.

"Dave," he said, "I'm going down to the emergency response center in the basement. I don't want you out on the street until I know more about what's going on. Come with me, but try to stay out of the way."

"Yeah, sure." Dave bit back the temptation to ask questions when he saw the set of his uncle's jaw.

Uncle Charlie's military face! Something big is going on, and I get to be on the inside of this emergency.

Glancing at his phone for messages and updates, Dave thought it odd that there were none, and returned the device to his pocket. He followed the older man as O'Reilly left the office, turned first toward the elevator, and then changed his mind, headed toward the nearest stairwell, and raced down the stairs, two at a time. Reaching the subbasement, O'Reilly entered a key code into a keypad. The door clicked as the lock disengaged. Dave kept pace as they hurried down the long corridor, and then passed through an open door into a large room.

Dave quietly slipped in behind his uncle and took a seat just inside the door at the back of the room. As he sat down, he glanced at his phone again. Still nothing. Two more people came in, and sat down at a bank of consoles facing a wall-sized display at the front of the room.

The buzz of conversation stopped as O'Reilly strode to the center of the room and approached a tall man in a white shirt. After a lengthy whispered conversation, O'Reilly turned to address the emergency response team, his expression grim.

"For those who have just arrived," he began, "there has been an explosion at the experimental area. Do we have any word on casualties?"

"No word on casualties," said a man wearing earphones.

"Is our nuclear power station still on line?"

"Yes," said the man, peering briefly at his monitor. "There was a power surge from the experimental area, but it didn't overload the safety systems, and power generation at the nuclear plant is nominal. That power surge ended abruptly at about the time of the explosion."

"Has the campus fire department been dispatched to the experimental field?"

"The first truck has just arrived. I'm in contact with Chief Gamble, but he needs a few minutes to assess the situation."

O'Reilly rubbed the scar on his chin. "Have we requested support from the mainland?"

"We've tried, but our communication links have been disrupted. We can't get through," said the communications technician.

"How can that be? Was every microwave tower knocked out?" exclaimed O'Reilly.

"I don't get it, either," answered the communications technician. "One of the towers is clear on the other side of the island and couldn't possibly have been affected by the explosion. I can reach the naval station on the south side of our island, but even they can't communicate with anyone on the mainland."

At least that explains my phone, thought Dave.

The wall display showed the firemen scurrying to deal with the blaze in the experimental area.

"Could you search the camera archives for the footage prior to the explosion?" asked O'Reilly.

"Yes, of course!" said the technician.

The video on the screen flashed backwards in time. The technician expertly froze the video frame at the point when the explosion had started, consuming part of the experimental field building.

"Go back two minutes and let's run forward," said O'Reilly.

The intact experimental field building appeared on the screen, surrounded by a spherical bubble shimmering faintly, like air over a ribbon of blacktop in hot desert sun. In the distance, the sky was blue, dotted with small cumulus clouds, but directly over the experimental building a black storm cloud was roiling violently.

The cloud grew more turbulent, and lightning flashes lit up the dark mass. Soon lightning began to hit the experimental building, and the shimmering bubble expanded rapidly outward, passing beyond the camera as the lightning strikes increased in intensity.

A short time later the explosion occurred, and the whole sky turned coal black. A moment later, like a television changing channels, a bright blue cloudless sky appeared, marred only by the black smudge of the explosion.

"Where did the clouds go?" someone asked.

The phone rang. "It's Professor Hoffstetter," said the communications technician, handing the phone to O'Reilly.

"Bertrand, are you all right?" O'Reilly asked. "What about the rest of your people?" O'Reilly's face gradually relaxed as he heard the answer.

"Calm down, Bertrand. What do you mean by 'have you seen the bridge?' What bridge are you talking about?"

O'Reilly listened for a few moments more, then cupped his hand over the mouthpiece and said to the technician controlling the view screen, "Ed, would you display the bridge to the mainland on the screen? Hoffstetter seems to think that something is the matter with the bridge."

The main screen shifted from a picture of fire trucks working at the explosion site to a view of the bridge to the mainland. Everyone gasped.

The bridge was only half there. The camera showed the familiar blacktop running in a smooth curve to the bridge at Causeway Point, only to end abruptly after a few hundred yards, as if sliced off by a knife. Five people had emerged from their vehicles and were pointing at the truncated end of the bridge. But it was not only the bridge. The mainland of North Carolina, only half a mile away twenty minutes before, had disappeared and been replaced by an unfamiliar shoreline that could be seen as a hazy shadow across miles of sea.

Dave was stunned. His heart raced, the room felt hot, and sweat beaded on his forehead. He had been following the accident with the detached excitement of a television viewer watching a disaster movie, but when the truncated bridge appeared on the screen, his mind reeled.

What's happened to the bridge?

O'Reilly, still holding the phone while staring over his shoulder at the main screen, was first to recover.

"I'll get back to you, Bertrand," he said softly into the mouthpiece and hung up.

"Where are the students now?" he asked in a deliberately calm tone. None of the staff answered. O'Reilly scowled at each person in turn. Every eye was transfixed on the amputated bridge.

"Where are the students now?" he asked in a louder tone. Still no one answered.

"Most would still be in class," answered Dave from the back of the room.

"Ken, get what's-his-name, the head of the campus patrol," ordered O'Reilly.

"That would be Ben Wychek," said the communications technician, tearing his eyes away from the bridge.

In a quiet voice O'Reilly continued, "Use the public address system. Tell the students we've had an explosion. It's under control, but for their safety, all classes are cancelled. They should clear the streets for the movement of emergency equipment, and return to their dormitories. Then call Ben Wychek and ask him to round up all the stragglers and get them back to their dorm rooms. For once I'm glad all of the students live on campus."

"Will do!" returned the communications technician. In a few moments his voice was blaring over the campus public address system at a volume so high they could hear the echo from a distant loudspeaker. The main screen shifted from campus camera to camera as the group clustered in the emergency response center watched the campus patrol begin to implement O'Reilly's most recent instructions.

"Go back to the camera observing the bridge," said O'Reilly.

"Yes," said the communications technician.

"Retrieve the footage from the archives, and roll the video from the point where the bridge is still intact."

In a few seconds they saw the bridge as it had been, spanning the strait. Nothing changed for some minutes. Occasionally a car crossed the bridge and headed toward the mainland.

"The explosion happened at 14:31, according to the other camera," said the technician.

The time counter at the bottom of the screen passed 14:30. Suddenly a curved, shimmering curtain appeared, passing the camera as it expanded across the bridge. As it did so, the whole screen turned coal black. In another moment, the blackness vanished and bright, clear blue sky appeared. The bridge was truncated, and the shoreline had receded.

The room was silent, deathly silent. The video clip ended, and the screen again showed the live video feed from the explosion site.

Dave saw another man, whom he recognized as Darwin Blackmore, the vice-chancellor, silently enter the room and approach O'Reilly. Blackmore was a tall, thin, impeccably dressed man with a sallow face ending in a goatee. He carried himself with the easy confidence of a man aware of his gifts and the power he wields.

"What seems to be the trouble, Charles?" he asked.

"Eh, what did you say?" said O'Reilly as he turned around and pulled his attention away from the video screen.

"What seems to be the trouble? Why were the students sent back to the dormitories?" repeated Blackmore, an icy edge to his voice.

His tone caused O'Reilly to give Blackmore a searching look. "I'll tell you what I know, Darwin. Hoffstetter was running a full-scale test of his force field generator as a run-up to the Department of Defense demonstration next month. Somehow, during the test, there was an explosion," he gestured to the screen, which was still centered on the experimental area. "But we have an even bigger problem. Show him the bridge!"

The bridge reappeared on the screen, truncated as before, except that a few more cars and people had gathered to stare at this concrete evidence for the unbelievable.

Blackmore was puzzled. "What am I looking at?"

"The bridge, man, the bridge to the mainland!" said O'Reilly, his voice rising.

"Oh my god!" said Blackmore, turning white as a sheet. "Where's the rest of the bridge? Where's the mainland…"

"Exactly!" said O'Reilly. "Darwin, you take over for me here."

"Where are you going?" asked Blackmore sharply.

"First I'm going to drive out and inspect the bridge myself, and then I'm going to the hospital to talk to Hoffstetter. I'll have to be able to give our people answers!"

With that he strode out of the room, beckoning Dave to follow. Using the same stairwell as before, they went up one floor to the first basement, and then to the underground garage.

Not given to ostentation, O'Reilly drove a small, well-used Toyota. The car emerged from the underground parking lot into bright sunlight, where smoke from the explosion, driven by the wind, formed a long, slanted column to the west. They drove slowly past the patrol cars of the campus police, who were already beginning to clear the streets, and headed for Causeway Point. There, more cars choked the approach to the bridge, and curious onlookers were gathered into groups, as if talking would shield them from the terrifying evidence of their senses.

Parking at the side of the road, O'Reilly and Dave got out of the car and walked past the groups of students to the bridge. The concrete structure, resting on large pillars buried in the ocean floor, seemed undamaged, extending ahead of them into the strait like the bowsprit of a ship. Fear gripped Dave's stomach as he walked out onto the bridge and saw the ocean, hundreds of feet below him. He tried not to think of the height but concentrated on putting one foot in front of the other.

After a couple of minutes, they approached the end of the pavement. O'Reilly, about ten feet ahead, continued to the very end of the bridge, where he crouched down on his hands and knees to examine the severed edge.

"Cut as cleanly as if with a sharp knife!" he muttered. "Not so much as an impact fragment."

Dave kept his eyes on his feet, determined not to betray his fear to his uncle. Suddenly the end of the bridge yawned before him, and he looked down into the foam flecked sea, churning against the last remaining bridge pillar at his feet. Dizziness and nausea washed over him. He would have toppled forward, but for the firm hand that pulled him back.

"Dave, don't stand so close. I don't want to have to explain to your mother…" O'Reilly didn't finish the sentence, but pulled Dave away from the edge. "Maybe you should sit down." Dave obeyed. O'Reilly looked at his nephew him for a moment with concern, and then returned to examining the bridge.

Uncle Charlie, we're both wondering when we're going to speak to my mother again. Where are we? How do we get back?

O'Reilly stood up. "Let's go back," he said in a subdued tone as he extended his hand and pulled Dave to his feet. They walked back to the car in silence, ignored by the clusters of people whose frightened, animated discussions buzzed in the background. Grateful his uncle didn't ask for an explanation of his behavior on the bridge, Dave left O'Reilly to his thoughts.

TWO

A New Beginning

From the bridge O'Reilly drove straight to the university hospital, now alive with frenzied activity in the aftermath of the explosion. Dave followed his uncle as he strode into the main foyer. The woman at the reception area was speaking frantically into the telephone. Her eyes widened when she recognized O'Reilly.

"I've really got to go!" she said to her caller, and hung up.

"Chancellor O'Reilly." The receptionist straightened her blouse and returned a recalcitrant wisp of hair to its rightful place.

"I need to see Professor Bertrand Hoffstetter right away. I understand he has been admitted."

The receptionist quickly tapped the name on her keyboard, hesitated a few seconds, then, "He's in room E-241. Down that hall to the end. Turn left to the elevator."

Thanking her, the two men hurried to follow her directions. The nurse at the station on the second floor of the E-wing showed them to Hoffstetter's room.

The door was slightly ajar. They could hear a muffled, repetitious sound coming from inside. They paused to listen. The indistinct sounds rose and fell in pitch like a chant.

O'Reilly glanced at Dave, and then rapped smartly on the door. The chanting stopped.

"Just a moment!" a gruff voice called out, then, "Who is it?"

By way of an answer, O'Reilly pushed the door wide and strode into the room. Dave followed. A portly man was just leaning over the far side of the bed. Dave saw him drop an angular, foot-long black object into a bag on the floor.

Hoffstetter's black hair was beginning to recede. In stark contrast to his hair, his beard and moustache were ash gray. His eyes were hard, trumping any joviality his corpulence might have conveyed.

O'Reilly offered a hand to Hoffstetter, who had recovered his sitting position in bed. "How are you, Bertrand?"

"Charles—I didn't expect to see you here. I'm fine, of course. I should be back at the experimental area, but these medical cretins insist on keeping me here under observation."

"What happened, Bertrand?"

"Who's he?" asked Hoffstetter sharply. Dave had again tried to make himself inconspicuous by quietly taking a chair at the foot of the bed.

"My nephew. He was in my office when the explosion hit." O'Reilly paused. "I want to keep him with me until I've had time to assess our situation. So what *has* happened, Bertrand?"

O'Reilly pulled a chair close to the bed, sat down, and leaned forward intently.

"Charles, I must tell you that I have made the most momentous discovery of my career," said Hoffstetter in a conspiratorial tone.

"What do you mean?" asked O'Reilly.

Hoffstetter looked at O'Reilly's face, as if trying to read his thoughts, and then continued. "I can say matter-of-factly, without prejudice or exaggeration, that I am the most brilliant physicist of my generation—arguably of all generations. But even I could not have predicted what happened today—"

"What *did* happen today?" interrupted O'Reilly.

Hoffstetter was annoyed at the interruption. "To put it simply, when I was powering up the Hoffstetter field generators"—he seemed to relish the sound of his own name—"the apparatus behaved erratically and eventually detonated."

"But you had tested this before! What was different this time?" asked O'Reilly.

"As far as I can tell," continued Hoffstetter, "in constructing the larger unit, we seem to have crossed a scale threshold of some sort. In all of the smaller experiments, the force field bubble appeared and could be controlled. This time, to put it as simply as I can, the field generators seemed to interact with the atmosphere and triggered an electrical storm, which overloaded the system. When the field collapsed..." Here he launched into unintelligible jargon.

O'Reilly put his hand up to stop the verbal deluge. "Bertrand, you're far beyond me. I need to understand this catastrophe in plain language so that I can communicate to the students and faculty. What do I tell them?"

"Don't you see, man? It wasn't a catastrophe; it was a breakthrough! I've made physics history! I deserve a second Nobel Prize..."

"Bertrand! What is 'it'? What has happened? Forget all this other crap."

"Do you know how the Hoffstetter force field generator works?" asked Hoffstetter petulantly.

"No!"

"The Hoffstetter force field causes a time lag or time shift inside the bubble. Oh, it's very small; it's in the range of about ten to the minus thirty-second of a second behind normal time, but that's enough to stop projectiles. Firing into the Hoffstetter force field is like trying to fire into yesterday—you just can't do it. At our time offset, air molecules and light can still tunnel through the time barrier. If I could draw 1,000 times more energy from the power plant, and if I had the equipment to increase the time offset, we could even stop the penetration of air molecules. An even larger time lag would stop radiation, such as light or even gamma rays."

"So how does that relate to what's happened?" asked O'Reilly.

"Charles, with due respect, you simply don't have the understanding to comprehend what happened. How can you expect me to explain it to you?"

"You need to try," said O'Reilly. "You can't drive us on a lee shore like this and then tell me it's too hard to explain."

"All right, all right," said Hoffstetter. "Give me a minute to decide how to explain it to you." Hoffstetter's eyes closed as he paused.

Dave's eyes wandered around the room. Next to Hoffstetter's bed on the floor was an open duffle bag. A jet-black obelisk jutted out of the bag. The obelisk, square in cross section and tapering to a pyramid at one end, had curious red letters on it in a script Dave did not recognize. He was just wondering about the nature of the object, and why Hoffstetter had appeared in such a hurry to put it away earlier, when Hoffstetter resumed his discourse.

"Think of it like this, Charles: electromagnetic radiation, such as light, has both frequency and intensity, which can be controlled separately. Frequency determines the color of the light. Intensity determines the brightness. Each can be modified independently. We have the same sort of control over the force field. The intensity determines the diameter of the force field bubble, and the frequency is analogous to the time offset. When the storm hit, it overloaded our intensity control and expanded the force field far beyond the experimental field. At some point in the expansion, the frequency control was also overloaded. First the time offset increased; then the force field collapsed precipitously as the generators exploded."

"That's why we saw the bubble expanding past our cameras, and when it turned black, that was the increase in the time offset?" asked O'Reilly, understanding beginning to dawn.

"Exactly!" declared Hoffstetter. "I can see my explanation's been clear."

"So what happened when the force field collapsed?" asked O'Reilly.

"Normally when the force field collapses, we return to our normal time. This time, however, the collapse of the very large time offset—we still don't know how large it was—did something to the matter inside the Hoffstetter field. Somehow it dislocated us; that is to say, it transported us to another place or perhaps another time. I don't know where."

"But that's preposterous!" exclaimed O'Reilly.

"Use your eyes! Use your head, man!" Hoffstetter shot back, sneering. "Where's the rest of the bridge? What happened to the mainland?"

"So where are we then?" asked O'Reilly, his eyes hardening at the contempt in Hoffstetter's voice.

"Well," said Hoffstetter, "let me work it out for you. The amputated bridge is incontrovertible evidence that Halcyon has moved. The alternatives are: we moved in space, we moved in time, or we moved right out of our space-time. Let me analyze these alternatives in turn. If we moved any great distance in space, Halcyon would be a small, airless, hemispherical asteroid drifting through space, the dead companion of our sun or some other distant sun. If we had been dislocated a shorter distance so that we remained on the surface of our planet, the sun would have been displaced in the sky at the time of our dislocation. I've run the video files. The clouds changed, but the sun remained exactly where it was in the sky. That may mean we've moved only a few miles, and that's why everything looks the same. The other part of the bridge is probably only a few miles away."

"If we had moved only a few miles," said O'Reilly, "the airwaves would be buzzing with communication, and a Coast Guard helicopter would have already arrived from the mainland. I don't think we've moved just a few miles! Remember the change in the cloud patterns? The weather doesn't change that much when one only moves a few miles. So what about your other alternatives?"

"I suppose," said Hoffstetter, "preposterous as it sounds, Halcyon could have moved forward or backward in time. That might explain the radio silence. If we moved to an earth in a parallel universe—"

"Backwards or forwards in time, parallel universe—are you serious?"

"Of course I'm serious!" snapped Hoffstetter. "Use your brain! Radio silence when there would be all kinds of squawking on all major frequencies—everything from short wave to radio to maritime communications. The sky changed, the shoreline has receded—how much more evidence do you need?"

Dave's head spun. He had the sensation of trying to escape from a trap. *This can't be true! This must be some kind of a joke. There must be a reasonable, logical explanation for this. Hoffstetter is a crackpot— no, he must have been injured by the explosion. They'll laugh about this tomorrow.* But in the back of Dave's mind there was the picture of the bridge, a phantom that wouldn't go away, a phantom that demolished every rationalization.

O'Reilly sat in stunned silence, and the silence became uncomfortably long. "How do we find out what's happened? How do we test these hypotheses?" asked O'Reilly at last in a weary voice.

"Well, if we're on the earth at a different time, we'll know when we examine the stars in the night sky. If we're on a sister earth in a parallel space-time, who knows what that may mean."

O'Reilly sat back in his chair by the bed and scowled. "Time travel seems pretty far-fetched, but since we don't know, let's hope for the best and plan for the worst. If we are displaced in time or in a parallel world, can we get back?" he asked grimly.

"I suppose, in principle," said Hoffstetter. "At least I could replicate the experiment and take us somewhere else if I had the equipment. But frankly I don't have a clue how to control this dislocation. There is no assurance that initiating another dislocation will take Halcyon home. Anyway, I have to assess the damage, and the sooner I can get out of here, the sooner I can begin."

"I see," said O'Reilly. He rubbed the scar on his chin and watched a nurse enter the room, deposit a tray of food on Hoffstetter's table, and leave. "I suppose our first order of business would be to figure out where we are. I'm going to talk to the staff in astronomy. What resources do you need to get us back?"

Dave saw the hint of a sly smile creep across Hoffstetter's face. "I'll need someone high up in the administration to help me get whatever resources I need. How about Blackmore? Can he be spared?"

"If that's what it will take," said O'Reilly evenly, "then you will have him to help you. Just get us home!"

Hoffstetter started to eat with appetite.

Why isn't Hoffstetter more upset? wondered Dave.

O'Reilly looked as if he was about to get up and leave, but changed his mind.

"How are the others?" said O'Reilly.

"Oh, my team is fine," said Hoffstetter absently, with a mouth full of food. "The control center is well protected, and the explosion didn't damage it. They have all of us here at the hospital only as a precaution."

"From what you said, you must have had some inkling that this experiment entailed some risk. How could you go ahead with it?" said O'Reilly, his exasperation growing.

"Of course there was some risk. We didn't know exactly what would happen if the field collapsed suddenly—that was one of the things we were going to test—but we knew there was a very small probability that if the field were to collapse precipitously, some unusual things might happen."

O'Reilly choked at the euphemism *unusual things*. "And shouldn't this have made you more cautious?" he sputtered.

Hoffstetter bristled. "Chancellor O'Reilly, it's easy to second-guess my decision after the fact. Without courage and a willingness to take risks, science cannot advance. Don't you know your history? You're a military man. Do you remember the Manhattan Project? Physicists had calculated that there was a low probability that the first atomic bomb explosion might set up a chain reaction in the atmosphere and destroy all life on our planet. But they conducted the test anyway because the need was great. I was faced with the same dilemma, and I didn't flinch from my duty to advance the cause of our knowledge and science." Hoffstetter bellowed for a nurse to adjust his pillow. No one came.

"How did you know about the bridge?" O'Reilly asked suddenly.

There was the slightest hesitation before Hoffstetter responded. "We have the same video camera links in the control room that you have in the emergency response center. The bridge happened to be up on one of the monitors, since we were keeping an eye on the weather from that quarter, so we saw the truncated bridge right away, after the field collapsed."

"Yes, yes, of course." O'Reilly sighed wearily. "I'd better be on my way." He motioned for Dave to follow. Once outside the room he shook his head in disbelief. "Somehow our intelligence and cleverness always outstrip our moral judgment and our good sense!" O'Reilly said, more to himself than to Dave. "Doing his duty to knowledge and science! I wonder what he's not telling me…"

As O'Reilly drove Dave back to his dormitory, Dave noticed his uncle's face looked drawn and gaunt in the afternoon light. He had aged several years in the space of a few hours. Dave thought about raising the question of the black obelisk in Hoffstetter's bag but decided now was not the time.

They arrived at a large multistory building with the name "Socrates" in bold relief above the doorway.

"Dave, I'm sorry to leave you like this. I know all this uncertainty about what's happened makes it very hard. But I need some time to make plans for Halcyon. Since I need to speak to the people here on our university television network tonight, I have to figure out how to come to grips with our situation. I need to think about a possible course for Halcyon that will bring us back home…or one that will at least let us survive."

"If anyone can get us out of this mess," said Dave, "it'll be you!" O'Reilly smiled for the first time since the explosion and squeezed Dave's shoulder affectionately. Dave started out of the car.

"One more thing, Dave. Please don't say anything to anyone until I've had a chance to make an announcement. I'll tell everyone tonight anyway. This accident and its implications will stretch the psychological fabric of our people to the limit. It's almost like telling them that their closest relatives have died. If this leaks out prematurely, we may have a riot on our hands before we can be ready for it."

Dave's mind was reeling as he walked up the stairs to his dorm room, checking his phone again, just in case. Of course, there was nothing. Fear hovered at the edge of his mind like a vampire bat. If he allowed it to settle, it would attach itself and suck the life out of him. *I've got to keep busy and not think about it.*

When he entered his dorm room, Glenn Thompson, his roommate, was sitting on his bed studying the topography of Miss Arizona.

"Hi, Dave!" Glenn said. "Hey – is your phone working?"

"Hi." Dave said without enthusiasm. "No, it isn't."

"That's weird. Neither's mine. Internet's down too. Must have something to do with the explosion. What's eating you?"

Dave evaded the question by asking another question. "What do you think about the explosion?"

"Well, it got me out of sociology today. Professor Aberhardt was continuing to rail against the twin social evils of religious fundamentalism and the nuclear family. I was glad to get a break. That class is a bore."

In an effort to stop thinking about the dislocation, Dave turned his attention to one of his favorite pastimes, baiting Glenn.

"Glenn, why are you spending so much time studying that skin magazine? Can't you get a real date?"

Glenn, who was used to this banter, feigned irritation. "As a matter of fact, I can get a date anytime I want. Sociology students are in great demand by the fairer sex. Women are social creatures, and that gives us a great advantage over social Neanderthals such as you engineers." He spat out the word *engineer* as if it were a disease rather than a discipline. "No," he continued, "Miss Arizona is a work of art, and she's low maintenance. Why shouldn't I enjoy her? Life is short, and I ought to get all I can in the time I have. So go for it! That's my motto."

Dave decided to escalate. "Glenn, when you sociologists think that women appreciate your social prowess, you're overlooking one important fact."

"What's that?"

"It's true sociologists are on the whole more sensitive and tenderhearted than engineers are."

"Yeah?" said Glenn suspiciously.

"Women relate well to you because they're beginning to mistake you for other women. Engineers, on the other hand, could never be mistaken for women, except for those who really *are* women, and if women are looking for real men with none of that warm wishy-washy milquetoast feeling about them, they turn to us."

Glenn's riposte was laced with expletives. The exchange ended with Dave hitting Glenn in the head with a small pillow he kept handy for just such an attack. After the errant return shot upended several books from the bookshelf next to his bed, Dave thought it was time to turn to something else. "Anything on TV?" he asked, turning on the set in their room. Only the university channel was broadcasting, and there was no programming except for a message saying that an important announcement was coming at 9:00 p.m. and everyone should tune in.

"I think I'll go downstairs to the store and buy a sandwich," said Dave, turning off the TV.

"Do you know when they'll let us out on campus again so we can go to the cafeteria to eat?" asked Glenn.

"No," said Dave, "that's why I'm going to get something now rather than wait for them to open the cafeteria."

"Always thinking about your stomach," groaned Glenn.

"Why don't you come down with me?" asked Dave.

"I told some of the guys I'd join them for supper," said Glenn, returning to his magazine.

As Dave left the dorm room he felt much better. He went down to the main floor that housed the dormitory store and sandwich outlet. But his mind kept going back to the accident, so he bypassed the store entrance, went outside and looked for the moon. It was a sliver, late in its last quarter and getting ready to set in the west, just as it should. Nothing seemed to have changed! He went back inside. There was only one other person in line ahead of him, a pretty brunette wearing a doctor's uniform. He caught sight of her nametag; it read "Pamela Lowental."

"Hi, Pam," said Dave as if he knew her.

"Oh, hi," said Lowental in a tone of familiarity. She looked at him closely. "Do I know you?"

"I don't think so," said Dave, "since I would have remembered you. Do you live in Socrates?"

"Yes, on the second floor."

"You're a doctor?"

"Nope, I'm a premed student."

At that moment a woman appeared from the back to give Lowental her order.

"See yah!" Pam said as she left with her food.

Dave nodded and smiled. It was his turn to order. He had just purchased two sandwiches, one for himself and one for Glenn, since he had doubts the cafeteria would open that day, when a campus patrol officer came in and asked the employees to close the store so he could talk to them.

Dave sat in the common area, looking out the large glass windows to the grass commons outside. The campus was deserted except for the occasional patrol car that passed in the street. He noticed that the officer who had closed the dorm store did not leave but stationed himself outside of the dormitory to enforce the curfew. Dave decided to go to the dorm weight room.

THREE

Mobilization

At 8:50 p.m. the campus public address system began urging everyone to turn on their televisions. Ten minutes later, Dave and Glenn watched the university station's broadcast as Chancellor O'Reilly and several other university dignitaries filed into the briefing room to face the cameras. Of particular interest to Dave was the presence of a naval officer, whom he did not recognize. O'Reilly came to the podium and looked squarely into the camera.

"This afternoon," he began, "a commissioning test of a new force field generator, carried out on behalf of the Department of Defense in our experimental area, had some serious and unintended consequences. The experiment triggered an electrical storm, which ultimately led to a detonation that damaged the force field equipment. Furthermore, unbelievable as it may seem, this explosion at 14:31 hours has dislocated—that is to say, moved—the whole island of Halcyon from its original location. We have not yet determined our new coordinates, but I can say that Halcyon's very best minds are working out our location and how to get back home.

"Let me tell you what we know. The air, the ocean, and even our preliminary astronomical data indicate that we have been dislocated to a part of the earth very close to our original position near North Carolina. It is puzzling that we have so far not been able to communicate with the mainland, but it is likely that the failure of our communication equipment is a consequence of the dislocation process."

"If this is a joke, it's a very bad joke!" sputtered Glenn as he jumped up from his chair.

"It's no joke," said Dave softly.

O'Reilly continued as a picture of the truncated bridge filled the screen. "The bridge to the mainland has been neatly sliced in two. Fortunately the whole island was dislocated, so all of our resources are intact. The nuclear power plant is still operational, and our self-contained island infrastructure is functioning well. We do not have to worry about running out of electricity, since there is enough nuclear fuel on site for about fifteen years.

"However, the geography around our island has changed. It is my belief, based on discussions with my advisors, that the island has moved only a few miles from its previous location. The coast is now six miles away. If we cannot reestablish communication with the mainland over the airwaves in the next few hours, then we will send a boat to the mainland.

"As I have said, our best evidence indicates that we have moved only a few miles. However, until we have confirmed this conjecture by communicating with the mainland, we must take steps to ensure the orderly functioning of our small community.

"As chancellor, I—together with the senate and Commander Sanderson from the naval station at the south end of the island—have taken it upon ourselves to form an interim government to ensure we continue to conduct our affairs in an orderly manner under the rule of law during this interregnum. It seems prudent under the circumstances to act as if we might be without communication or support for a protracted period of time. We will work to assure our basic necessities. Once we have taken steps to ensure our survival, if we have neither been rescued nor found a way to return home, then we will hold elections and operate as a freely democratic country.

"For now we will declare martial law. All food will be used to carry our population through the next critical few weeks. There will be no hoarding. I repeat, all food will be shared equally. If we have to go hungry, we will all go hungry together. In addition to the 15,000 students housed in dormitories on campus, we have about 5,000 faculty and support personnel. Many of these support personnel lived on the mainland. They will be housed mostly with the faculty in the faculty district, but some will also have to be placed in your dormitory rooms. If you have a large room and must accept a third person, please do so with goodwill.

"Finally, you will ask, 'What are our next steps?' To that I would respond that our most immediate need is food. We must look first to the sea to support us. Securing our food supply will buy us the time we need to reverse the dislocation or await rescue. To buy us this time, I am suspending all classes, and we will assign everyone to necessary tasks. It is essential that we work together and put our community ahead of our own personal wants and needs. It is only by this kind of unselfishness that we will pull through this crisis. May God have mercy on us!" O'Reilly took a sip of water from a glass and cleared his throat.

"We are all asking what has happened to us. Dr. Blackmore, the vice-chancellor, and his team of physicists and engineers will take personal responsibility for investigating the accident. I have asked him to keep us informed of his progress on an ongoing basis.

"I will take personal responsibility for our survival. I have asked Trevor Huxley, who will take responsibility for food procurement, to provide some of the details on logistics. Trevor?"

Huxley, a short, heavily jowled, overweight man with a red face, took off his glasses to clean them. His voice was unexpectedly thin and reedy, despite his flabby appearance, as he read from a prepared speech. "I am sure that everyone is as shocked as I am at what has happened. I'm sure you will understand me if I say that we must all pull together. What I say may seem high-handed to some, but it is essential to our survival."

Dave saw O'Reilly shift uncomfortably at the longwinded preamble. Huxley noticed the motion, cleared his throat, and applied himself to the written text. "It is essential that we keep all the critical departments functioning: engineering, the physical sciences, and medicine. We will also give priority to the support functions that keep our buildings lit and infrastructure operative. This will mean that additional personnel with the right expertise will have to contribute. If you are asked to lend a hand or take a shift, I would ask that you do so.

"We hope, of course, that we will be rescued soon, but it would be wise and prudent to act as if we might be cut off from home for some time. As the chancellor has pointed out, our critical need is food. We estimate that we have about two weeks worth of food in storage. If we ration it carefully and collect all of the food in the various campus stores, we may have enough for three weeks.

"Those of you who are not directly seconded to the critical support activities that I have already mentioned will be asked to perform one of three functions, and we will assign these by dorm. First, every available boat will be used to bring fish back to campus. We will convert one of the warehouses at East Harbor into a fish processing plant. The dorms Aristotle, Aquinas, Bacon, Bentham, Descarte, Fuerbach, Hegel, Hobbes, Kant, Locke, Machiavelli, and Mill are on fish procurement duty.

"Second, dorms Nietsche, Peirce, Plato, Sartre, Spinoza, and Voltaire will lend support to our experimental farms and harvest the food that we have in the ground, planting new crops if necessary.

"Finally, the dorms Schopenhauer and Socrates have been designated to travel to the mainland.

"If you are contacted by one of the departments to contribute your particular skill, please do so. Otherwise, please contribute to the assignment given to your dormitory. The senate respectfully asks that you provide your full support."

So my dorm is assigned to exploration. I wonder if Uncle Charlie had me in mind when he made that choice.

O'Reilly approached the microphone and nodded curtly to Huxley. "One more thing," said O'Reilly. "The naval station at the south end of the island will be considered a critical university department and will be responsible for the defense of the island. Commander Sanderson is now officially in charge of the campus patrol, and he is now also a member of our senate. I believe he would like to say a few words. Commander Sanderson."

Sanderson, a broad shouldered man in his mid-forties with short hair graying around his temples, strode briskly to the podium. "In view of the seriousness of our situation," Sanderson said, "as part of the martial law Chancellor O'Reilly has already announced, a curfew at 21:00 hours—that is 9:00 p.m.—is now in force. Please return to your dormitory rooms by that hour. That's all that I have to say at this time."

The broadcast went off the air, replaced by a message saying that regular programming would resume the next evening at 7:00 p.m.

Glenn was so angry he stormed out of the room. Dave rose from his chair and began pacing. Ever since the sight of the bridge and the interview with Hoffstetter, he had been trying to explain away the evidence for the dislocation. The official announcement robbed him of the solace of denial, and he was angry.

Why am I angry? If we have been dislocated, why blame them for telling me?

One thing had surprised Dave. He had never heard Uncle Charlie refer to God before. At Halcyon, reference to God was regarded as unscholarly, unprofessional, and anachronistic. Certainly, there was more than one side to Uncle Charlie.

I wonder what other surprises this crisis situation might yet reveal?

Dave's thoughts were interrupted when Glenn stormed back into the room. "No way am I going to be ordered around," snarled Glenn. "I know my rights. I don't have to do anything." He picked up the phone, changed his mind, and slammed the receiver back onto the cradle.

"Look, Glenn," said Dave, "we don't really know where we are or how much trouble we're in. Wouldn't it make sense to cooperate?"

"I know how these military guys think," continued Glenn. "The first hint of an emergency comes along, and they go on a power trip, declare martial law, and begin ordering everyone around. I want no part of it."

When he saw the anger in Glenn's face Dave knew that Uncle Charlie had been right. If there were more like Glenn, then the university stood on the brink of a riot. *Oh boy, I don't think I've heard the end of this. I hope this doesn't lead to trouble!*

The rest of the evening was spent in small groups in the dorm common area. The group seemed evenly split: there were those who, like Glenn, were angry, those who denied the whole thing, explaining it away as a practical joke or a colossal misunderstanding and those whose fear was palpable.

About midnight, despite the curfew, Dave went out into the dorm courtyard. He realized that even though he had argued for cooperation, the imposition of a curfew rankled him. He looked up and saw the Big Dipper and Polaris. Nothing seemed to have changed. If they had been displaced in time by 50,000 years, he remembered from astronomy class that the Big Dipper handle would be distorted. If it weren't for the bridge and the mainland, he would think his parents were still only a phone call away. He sat outside looking at the stars until 1:00 a.m. They made him feel as if he were home.

FOUR

Fish Tales

Al Gleeson had had a sinking feeling something was seriously wrong ever since he'd heard the call to return to his dorm room. Now the television broadcast he was watching confirmed it.

Lord, what do I do now? What do we all do now?

Al ran his hand through his hair and turned to his roommate, Brendon Monk. Brendon had the pasty white complexion of a man in shock.

"Are you all right, Brendon?"

"I don't believe it! I don't believe it! This can't be happening," said Brendon, clenching and unclenching his fists. They could hear the buzz of animated conversation as students on the fifth floor of Socrates left their rooms, chattering in the hallway about the news. Al and Brendon were just going to join them when Al's phone rang.

"Hello," said Al as he watched Brendon head out into the hallway.

"Did you watch the news?" asked a familiar voice.

It was Tom Chartrand, a close friend. "Can you believe it?" said Al, by way of affirmation.

"I don't know what to believe," continued Tom. "Listen, this isn't a good time, but I have to ask a favor."

"What is it?" asked Al.

"I just got a phone call from Sturgeon, my biology prof, and he's asked me and a bunch of the other students from my class to help him with today's catch. He's been out in a trawler with his grad students since the classes were cancelled, bringing in whatever fish he could find, and he needs help sorting and classifying the catch. Since you are the fount of all wisdom and a fisherman by hobby, I thought I'd ask you to come along and lend your prodigious talent to this exercise."

Tom's optimism was good medicine. Al jumped at the chance to get away. "Your unabashed flattery has won the day. I'd like nothing better right now than to get out of the dorm and do something useful."

"Okay, I'll meet you downstairs. Wear your old clothes; you're going to be a mess when you get back."

Al changed and headed downstairs. Tom was waiting for him; together they left the building and began the walk to East Harbor, about three quarters of a mile away. A short way from the dormitory they were stopped by a campus patrolman.

"What are you guys doin' out after curfew?" he growled.

"My name is Tom Chartrand, and this is Al Gleeson. We've been seconded to biology, and I just received a call to go to East Harbor to help unload a catch of fish."

"Who are you working for?" asked the officer in a suspicious voice.

"We're to report to Professor Sturgeon in biology. He took out a trawler this afternoon and has just arrived back."

"Wait here!" The officer walked out of earshot and spoke at length on his communicator. Al saw him keep his eyes fixed on them as if he expected them to make a run for it.

The patrolman ambled back. "Okay, you're good to go! Your story checks out. Here, take these passes and show them to any other patrolmen you meet so you don't waste their time reporting in. You're supposed to have these before you head out." He scrawled a signature on a couple of pieces of green paper and shoved the passes into their hands. "Fill in the blanks later."

After about twenty minutes they arrived at East Harbor. The quay was deserted except for one lone trawler. A huge tube from the hold of the trawler was spewing fish onto a tarp on the wharf.

"Professor Sturgeon!"

A figure cloaked in rainwear turned toward him. "Oh, hello, Chartrand! Glad you could make it. Can you believe it! I've been trawling off these waters for more than ten years, and this is the first time I've run into a school of fish like this. I filled up the whole hold in four hours!"

Al studied the professor. In addition to his rain gear, Sturgeon had fine chainmail gauntlets on his hands, like a butcher's cutting gloves. He was bearded, and his head was framed by bushy long hair that made him look like a bear in his hood. A hook-like nose protruded from the hairy shrubbery of his face, which was broken only by a smile that revealed crooked teeth. His eyes were a contrast to his austere face and showed an uncommon friendliness. Al's interest was piqued by the conversation.

"Normally, it would take me a week of trawling to catch what I caught today in an afternoon," said Sturgeon. "You know what else is funny?"

"No, what?"

Sturgeon picked a couple of fish from the mound. "Not only did we catch a lot quickly, but look at these. We have a lot of species mixed in together." At this point he noticed Al examining the fish. "Who's your friend?" he asked, pointing at Al.

"Let me introduce Al Gleeson. He's a fisherman by hobby and has come along to help."

"Glad to meet you!" said Sturgeon, affably taking off his gauntlet to shake Al's hand. "Please help me sort the species into piles so we can make a tally. If you need any help identifying a particular fish, ask one of the grad students. I'm afraid I'm going to have to go back to supervise the discharge. Use gloves. Some of the fish have spines. There's a pile of spares on that box." He waved in the general direction of a forklift, then turned and bellowed instructions to a student standing on the deck of the trawler.

Al followed Tom as he picked up two pairs of gloves. They got to work on opposite sides of the enormous mound of fish. Al pulled two large Atlantic mackerel out of the pile. Indeed it looked like his area was mostly mackerel. He found a large tarp that already had several hundred mackerel on it, and added his to the growing pile. He found the occasional black sea bass in among the mackerel. It gave him an odd sense of security since he had often caught black bass off Halcyon near the causeway bridge, when he could get away for an early morning fishing trip.

On his third trip back, he saw the tail of what looked like a small black-tipped shark sticking out of the pile. He carefully gave it a pull. It didn't budge. He pulled harder, and the pile began to shift as the fish came out.

It can't be! I don't believe it. His mind reeled as he looked at the forty-pound monstrosity he was holding by the tail. The fish was about three feet long with the dorsal and tailfins of a small shark. But instead of the jaws and head of a shark, he saw a mass of ten tentacles crowning the creature's head like the snake hair of a Medusa.

Al let the bizarre creature slide to his feet, and then stood there dumbfounded, looking down at the jumble of tentacles. One of the graduate students brought Professor Sturgeon over.

"May I have a look?" he asked gravely. He bent down and grabbed the heavy fish by the tentacles using both hands and spread them to reveal a blunt shark's mouth with razor sharp teeth.

"I've never seen anything like this before," he muttered. He flexed the fish torso. "It's clearly a chordate. How can this be? Where are we? What's happened to us?" He looked around at the gathering crowd. "Just an unusual specimen," he said in a loud voice. "Please get back to work. We don't want to be here all night."

Exhausted and covered in scales and fish oil, Al and Tom walked back to the dorm. Although most of the fish had been familiar Atlantic species, there must have been two dozen examples of species that Al had never seen before.

"So what happened back there?" asked Tom at last, breaking the silence.

Al drew a deep breath and ran his hands through his hair. "From what I can tell," said Al slowly, "Halcyon is not just a few miles from our former location, as O'Reilly was hoping. We found a good many fish tonight that, as far as I can tell, have never been reported off North Carolina, or anywhere else on Earth. Sturgeon said as much."

"What are you saying?" asked Tom, a current of fear in his voice.

"I do not think the senators were quite accurate in their assessment," said Al. "When we travel to the mainland, I do not know what we're going to find, but I do not think it will be North Carolina."

The Halcyon Dislocation is available for purchase online as a trade paperback or in common e-book formats at Wolfsburg Imprints: http://WolfsburgImprints.com/
Also available through Word Alive Press, Amazon, Barnes&Noble, Indigo Chapters or through your favorite bookseller.

About the Author

The Halcyon Dislocation is Peter Kazmaier's first novel. In writing this work he has been able to pursue a life-long dream of writing fast-paced novels that explore the intersection between adventure, science, faith and philosophy.

J. R. R. Tolkien's *Lord of the Rings*, C. S. Lewis' *The Chronicles of the Narnia*, and Stephen R. Lawhead's trilogy, *Song of Albion* and Robert Jordan's *Wheel of Time*™ are among his favorite and best-loved books. He also very much enjoys science fiction classics such as Robert Heinlein's *Tunnel in the Sky*.

Dr. Kazmaier has spent most of his scientific career as a research scientist in industry and also has been an Adjunct Professor of Chemistry at Queen's University since 1999. He has published more than sixty scientific articles in refereed journals and was awarded the Arthur K. Doolittle award for Best Paper by the American Chemical Society in 1993. Cited as the inventor or co-inventor on more than 175 patents, his strong background in science enables him to bring authentic scientific insight to *The Halcyon Dislocation*.

Dr. Kazmaier joined the American Chemical Society in 1976, and the Chemical Institute of Canada in 1980, The Word Guild in 2004.

He was married to Kathryn in 1976 and they live in Mississauga near Toronto. They enjoy spending time at their cottage near Seeley's Bay, Ontario on the Rideau Canal.

Books by Peter Kazmaier

The Halcyon Dislocation
Questioning Your Way to Faith

Acknowledgements

Honest, heartfelt, one-on-one conversations on important topics—perhaps over a beer or a cup of coffee—are one of the delights of my life. The errors and shortcomings of this book are entirely my own, but whatever is good and helpful surely originates in many of these delightful exchanges.

Editors, it seems to me, rarely get the acknowledgment they deserve for trimming an ungainly, overly loquacious tome into something readable, coherent, and lucid. Patricia Paddey has not only supported this work from the outset, but much that is good in this book is due to her diligent ministrations.

This book would likely never have come into being if Mike Burns had not argued for a book that emphasized the importance of the "big question" dialogue in *The Halcyon Dislocation*. It was at his urging and encouragement that *Questioning Your Way to Faith* really began to take shape. His insightful questions, based on years working with youth, helped me to hone my arguments and fill gaps in the treatment.

My monthly writer's group, "The Egglestonians," led by Don Martin, helped to smooth the rough edges of my writing. Particular thanks are due to Bonnie Beldan-Thomson, Brian Meyer, Zinta Meyer, and Ian MacLeod for their constructive comments on this manuscript.

Tricia Sheridan, author *Magdahlia's Medallion*, spent many hours refining the text of *Questioning Your Way to Faith*, bringing her author's gaze to bear on the characters, the dialogue and working to bring a unity to the whole I couldn't achieve on my own. Many thanks!

I am grateful to my long-time friend from my days in graduate school, John Greenhorn, for his thorough reading of the manuscript and his many insightful questions on the points I was trying to make. He often saw third alternatives to positions I initially perceived as binary.

Mark Jokinen is another friend I have known since graduate school. His love of books, his love for the truth, and his insatiable desire to really 'know' have been an inspiration to me. In our conversations, he has always pushed me to go beyond the surface to the data, and to think through positions for myself without taking someone else's word for it. He constantly challenged me not to make a "straw man" of the atheist positions presented by Floyd. To the degree that I have succeeded, I owe my thanks to Mark.

Zoran Popovic is a renowned physicist, colleague, and friend. We disagree on many of the questions discussed in this book, but he has always modeled for me the attitude of respectful dialogue and thoroughgoing data-based analysis. We always agreed that we were both looking for the truth and that was our common starting point.

I had the privilege of spending six months with Professor Roald Hoffmann at Cornell University. Although we spoke mostly about chemistry and did not speak much about our disagreements on worldview, his generosity, his openness for respectful dialogue, and his courage in championing the cause of the oppressed profoundly impressed me. His ability to respectfully engage people who disagreed with him—whether on chemistry or worldview—were valuable in helping me recognize the importance of respectful dialogue with those with whom we disagree.

Rick Wukasch and Matt Vincent, my pastors at The Meeting House in Mississauga, have been a source of great encouragement in writing this book. Under their tutelage, many of these questions came up in our Jesus 101 courses, a safe forum in which inquirers and interested skeptics could ask any question they wished about the nature and existence of God and what it means to become a Christ-Follower. These challenging questions were instrumental in helping me think through them, and also in developing illustrations for making the answers understandable.

I am also grateful to be under the regular teaching of Bruxy Cavey, the Teaching Pastor at The Meeting House. His messages have challenged my thinking and many of Al's arguments are undoubtedly flavored with Bruxy's approach to these questions. His openness to questions and his willingness to acknowledge when he doesn't know the answer is refreshing.

Some of the most instructive conversations I have had occurred as part of a book club that I attend with my wife Kathy, Dwight and Hope Strong and Doug and Patricia Paddey. As we read a broad range of thought-provoking books and discuss their spiritual implications, I receive a lot of nourishment. Thank you for the excellent food and conversation.

The questions at the end of the book were vetted by a group of men at an annual outing I host at our cottage. I'm grateful to Frank Lembo, Andy Quinn, Bert Renkin, and Willie Wise for their help in improving the discussion questions at the end of the dialogue.

I thank my greater family for their willingness to tolerate disagreement and the many passionate discussions we have had that I trust have served to strengthen our quest for the truth.

Finally I thank The Lord Jesus Christ, the Ultimate Reality, whose light has helped me to make sense of this world and the people in it, whose light has shown purpose in a world that was without Him dark, insipid, and meaningless. May this book, despite all of its defects, bring glory to His name and encourage readers above all to become Truth-Seekers, wading through the propaganda, derision, and subtle coercion that seems to be the inevitable response of our secular society to any faith position that claims to be seeking the truth, until my readers (as is my hope) find The Ultimate Reality.

www.ingramcontent.com/pod-product-compliance
Lightning Source LLC
Chambersburg PA
CBHW060427260626
47161CB00005B/1818